"Are you saying I can't take care of my own daughter, Nick?"

"*Our* daughter, Josie. You need to remember I'm a part of her life now."

"You didn't know she existed until I told you."

Nick frowned. "She's still my responsibility. Your stubborn pride is getting in your way."

"This has nothing to do with pride." She pushed away from him and stared out the kitchen window. "You had no right to stick your nose in where it didn't belong."

"Would you listen to yourself? This has everything to do with pride, Josie. You're so bent on doing everything for yourself that you won't let me step in to help. What's the big deal?"

She gritted her teeth and glared at him. "I didn't ask for your help."

"No, because you think you have to carry every burden by yourself." He gentled his voice. "When are you going to look around and see how much people care about you?"

Why couldn't he understand she couldn't count on anyone but herself?

Books by Lisa Jordan

Love Inspired

Lakeside Reunion
Lakeside Family

LISA JORDAN

has been writing for over a decade, taking a hiatus to earn her degree in early childhood education. By day, she operates an in-home family child-care business. By night, she writes contemporary Christian romances. Being a wife to her real-life hero and mother to two young adult men overflow her cup of blessings. In her spare time, she loves reading, knitting and hanging out with family and friends. Learn more about her at www.lisajordanbooks.com.

Lakeside Family

Lisa Jordan

Love Inspired

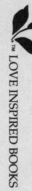

™ LOVE INSPIRED BOOKS

ISBN-13: 978-0-373-87762-1

LAKESIDE FAMILY

Copyright © 2012 by Lisa Jordan

www.LovelnspiredBooks.com

Printed in U.S.A.

May the God of hope fill you with all joy
and peace as you trust in him, so that you may
overflow with hope by the power of the Holy Spirit.
—*Romans* 15:13

For Lilly, my sunshine. You are the light of my blueberry. And the light of my heart. Thank you for teaching us what special really means. For Lynn and Woody—when God chose parents for Lilly, He couldn't have made a finer match. You are my heroes.

For Your glory, Lord. Without You, none of this is possible.

Acknowledgments

Michelle Lim, brainstorming queen, whom I have the pleasure to call friend and critique partner, thank you for helping me uncover Josie's story. Your brilliance dazzles me.

Kym Mullins, your sacrificial gift gave someone another chance at life. You are a blessing, friend. Thank you for sharing your experience.

Kathy Hurst and Lon Hurst, thank you for the ambulance photos and information about EMTs. Any mistakes are mine.

Dr. Amy Lindberg, thank you for sharing information about the National Marrow Donor Program. More than that, I treasure your friendship.

Dr. Ronda Wells, thank you again for your medical wisdom. Any mistakes are my own.

Dr. Reba J. Hoffman and Beth K. Vogt, thank you for your wisdom and red pens.

Susan May Warren and Rachel Hauck—Josie and Nick survived the Circle of Insecurity. Thanks for your amazing mentorship and consistent faith in me!

Rachelle Gardner, my wonderful agent, and Melissa Endlich, my wonderful editor, thank you for believing in me and teaming to help share my books with readers. Thank you to the rest of the Love Inspired team for your hand in bringing my book to print.

As always, thank you to Patrick, Scott and Mitchell. Your continued support and encouragement inspire me to keep writing. I love you forever.

Chapter One

Josie had spent the past ten years trying to forget Nickolas Brennan existed. And now she needed him more than ever.

Hard to believe after all this time he worked less than two hours from where she lived.

She climbed out of her car, slammed the door and pulled her wool coat tighter. Flipping up the collar to ward off the chill slithering down her spine, Josie slid her purse over her shoulder and trudged through the slushy parking lot toward Twain Hall. The aged brick building, which housed the English department, crested a small knoll with a familiarity to the campus as worn leather patches on a tweed blazer.

Freezing rain stung her cheeks as she waited at the corner for a snow plow to lumber past, leaving a trail of salt on the icy blacktop.

She'd give up her family's secret Italian doughnut recipe to be lying on a tropical beach somewhere. Anywhere. Didn't matter as long as sun, sand and surf were involved. And she and Hannah could build sand castles that withstood the constant crashes of life's harsh realities.

Someday.

She hurried across the street and stared at Twain Hall,

with its arched stone doorway and faded redbrick exterior. Evergreen shrubs lipped the building. Two stout trees guarded the wide steps, their bare limbs hunching over the sidewalk, bearing winter's burden.

No going back now.

Passing through the double doors, she paused to wipe her wet feet on the nubby industrial mat. The scent of disinfectant scorched her throat. Varnished wood molding, walls painted the color of aged parchment and gleaming tile floors greeted her. Photos in heavy wooden frames of men and women wearing stern expressions eyed her from the opposite wall as she passed by. Was Nick's picture among them? She didn't stop to check.

Upholstered chairs clustered around a circular table dotted with Starbucks cups where a small group of students gathered. Several balanced open laptops while leafing through textbooks and scribbling in notebooks. One guy lounged with his stretched-out legs crossed at the ankles and head back. His snores bounced off the frosted windows.

A woman, who appeared to be a little older than the other students, sat away from them, but watched with a wistful expression on her face. Josie caught her gaze and smiled, totally understanding how it felt to be on the outside of the circle.

While her friends had shopped for homecoming gowns and pedicures, Josie had bought maternity clothes and put together a nursery. Forget about graduation. Too humiliated to return to school, she had begged her father to homeschool her during her senior year. Her diploma came in the mail.

Josie shelved the memory and focused on her reason for being on campus. She followed the signs to the office and nearly choked on the floral perfume that saturated the air.

A young woman with straight salon-highlighted hair and wearing a black-and-silver Linwood Park Knights hoodie stood behind a counter, texting on her cell phone. Seeing Josie, she closed her phone and tucked it into the back pocket of her skinny jeans. "May I help you?"

Josie closed her fingers around the scrap of paper with Nick's office address, gripping it as if it were a lifeline. "I'm, uh, looking for Dr. Brennan."

"He's not in." The girl, probably a work-study student, pulled out her phone as if to say their conversation was over.

Not so fast, honey.

She should've called. But she couldn't risk him refusing to see her. He *had* to say yes. *Had to.*

Josie peeled off her turquoise leather gloves and shoved them in her coat pocket. "Do you know when he will be back?"

"He has class on Monday at eight." She blew a pink bubble and popped it, not even bothering to look up from her texting.

She couldn't wait until Monday. She needed to talk to him now.

Josie gripped the edge of the counter and fought to keep her voice calm. "Is there a way to reach him?"

"Leave him a voice mail, I guess."

"I really need to talk to Dr. Brennan." Josie cringed at the desperation seeping into her voice. She paused a second to regroup. "If I leave my number with you, would you call him and ask him to contact me as quickly as possible?"

"I guess." Again, she didn't bother looking up from where her thumbs danced across the keypad.

Josie balled her hands to keep from reaching over the counter and snatching the phone out of the girl's hands. "You guess? Listen, *honey.* Talking with Dr. Brennan is about the last thing on my want-to-do list for today, but my daughter's life depends on it. So, how about if you stow your phone along with your snotty attitude and *try* to be a little helpful?"

Campus Barbie rolled her eyes. She closed her phone and shoved it into her back pocket. She flashed a toothpaste commercial smile. "How can I *help* you?"

If she didn't need to see Nick so badly, she'd tell the girl exactly how she could help. But Hannah depended on her.

Josie pulled out a business card, scribbled her cell phone number on the back and slid it across the counter. "He can reach me at this number—day or night. Please contact him and have him call me as quickly as possible."

The girl took her card and nodded toward an older woman wearing a navy suit sitting at a computer with a phone cradled on her shoulder. "I'll give it to Irene. I have to head to class in ten minutes."

Josie forced a smile of thanks and strode out of the office, her leather boot heels clicking against the tile. She headed for the front door, passing the row of framed staff photos, then paused. Scanning the faces, she searched for Nick's. Had he changed much in the past decade?

There. Bottom left. Out of all the photos, he was the only one smiling. Glare from the overhead lights reflected off the glass, blocking a good look at his face. She glanced over her shoulders. Seeing no one in the corridor, she stretched on her tiptoes and pulled his picture down.

With one shoulder leaning against the wall, she stared at his face, turning back time to her junior year when he'd meet her at her locker, sling an arm over her shoulder and walk her to class. After classes, they'd hang out in the school newspaper office and work on the *Ridgefield Review.*

She traced a finger over the glass covering the one-dimensional image of the only man she loved enough to hand over her heart. He returned it in pieces before he left for college, claiming it was for the best.

Yeah, for him.

"I don't think those are to take."

A deep voice corded with humor startled her. She hadn't heard anyone walking behind her. Heat scalded her throat at getting caught staring at her past.

She jerked away from the wall and stretched to hook the frame back on its anchor. The picture caught on the nail. She dropped her hand only to watch the slow-motion descent of the frame smashing to the floor.

"Oh, no!" She crouched and picked up the frame. Cracks webbed from corner to corner, covering his face. A piece of the wood broke off and skittered across the floor. The man trapped it under his polished black loafer.

Josie wanted to pull her coat over her head and scurry out of the building. Unfortunately life taught her that running from her problems solved nothing.

She stood, refusing to make eye contact with the guy until her face no longer resembled the strawberry smoothie she'd sucked down that morning. Gripping the picture, she turned to face him.

And nearly dropped the frame.

The man standing in front of her with hair the color of her finest Columbian roast and chocolate-drop eyes crinkling around the edges like her homemade snickerdoodles mirrored the image pressed under the cracked glass. And that smile. It could melt the frosting off her homemade éclairs. For a second, the warmth in his eyes made her feel safe.

Instead of a black-and-white Ridgefield Panthers letterman jacket and jeans, he wore a black suit, white dress shirt and blue-and-green diamond-patterned tie. The lanky boy she had fallen in love with over ten years ago had matured into a man who had the potential to break her heart all over again.

"Nick." His name came out as a gasp. Her heart raced.

"Yes, but most of my students call me Dr. Brennan." He took the frame from her hands and shook his head. "It's official. I've cracked."

Didn't Campus Barbie say he was out?

"I'm, ah, not one of your students." She swallowed back the rest of her words. She couldn't blurt out her reason for coming. Not here in the middle of the hall. She pulled out her gloves and slowly slipped them on, hoping to warm her suddenly chilled fingers.

"Oh, sorry. I just assumed you were a student. Do you make it a habit of removing pictures from walls?"

Was he laughing at her?

"What? No. I just…" What could she say? She wanted a better look at the man who broke her heart? A better look at the man she desperately needed to save her daughter's life?

He glanced at his watch then the door, as if he had to be someplace. "I was just kidding. I'll take this back to my office and get it fixed. I need to head out to an appointment. Watch out for falling photographs." He walked backward a few steps, sent her another one of those dazzling smiles, then rotated on his heel to head back to his office.

"Wait." She hurried to catch up with him, trying not to let the fact that he didn't recognize her weigh down her heart.

Nick stopped and turned. His eyes swept over her. He stiffened. She saw the second recognition lit the lightbulb inside his head. A slow smile spread across his face. "Josie Peretti."

Her stomach shimmied. Only Nick could make her name flow like melted caramel.

"You look amazing."

"Thanks. Listen—"

"I'd love to stay and catch up, but I really must run. I'm late for an appointment."

She fished through her purse for another business card, took ten precious seconds to scrawl her cell phone number on the back and thrust it at him. "Please call me after your appointment. It's important. Please."

Nick glanced at the card, then tucked it in the inside pocket of his suit jacket. "Okay. I'll do that."

Josie's shoulders sagged as he disappeared into his office. Would he follow through? The Nick she knew once upon a time was always true to his word. She had no idea who he had become.

But it had to be enough.

Okay, God, you opened the door. Please push him through. For Hannah.

Heart thrumming, she hurried back to her car and unlocked it with the remote. As soon as it chirped, she wrenched the door open, hurled herself behind the wheel and slammed the door. She drew in several deep breaths.

If it weren't for Hannah, she'd walk away and not look back. But it didn't matter what skeletons the past held, she needed to dig them up to save her daughter's life.

Her phone rang constantly when she barely had time to breathe, but when she wanted…hoped for a call, it remained silent.

With her back pressed against the stainless-steel counter, Josie pulled her phone out of her pocket, checking for the hundredth time to see if the ringer was turned up, or if a call had come in but she'd missed it.

Volume was fine.

No calls.

Focus on something else.

She sighed, shoved the phone into her pocket and pulled on two pink pig-shaped oven mitts before reaching into the oven for the browned blueberry muffins. She set the pan on top of the stove next to a cooling apple pie. Sweet sugar scents danced with the spicy cinnamon. Reaching for the baking sheet lined with rows of scooped chocolate chip cookie dough, she slid it in the oven, closed the door and set the timer.

Agnes Levine, her assistant manager, breezed through the swinging kitchen door, leaving a fragrant trail of perfume behind her. With mugs dangling from her ringed fingers, she balanced a stack of plates and set them in the dishpan next to the sink. "Dining room's cleared, Sugar Pie."

"Thanks, Agnes."

Agnes pulled the apron over her head and hung it on the hook by the industrial-size stainless side-by-side refrigerator. "No call yet?"

"Not yet. Guess I'll have to call the department on Monday. I can't afford to drive all the way out there again." Josie filled the deep sink with soapy water and added a splash of bleach.

"You think Sorority Sally passed on the message?" Josie's lips twitched at Agnes's nickname for the student in Nick's office. "Campus Barbie? I hope so. We're running out of time."

"How's Hannah doing?"

"Same. Tired, but still keeps smiling." Josie pulled on a pair of yellow gloves and stuck her hand in one of the glass mugs. She stared out the window at the smudged sky of mauve hues blended with lavender and gray. The same colors as Hannah's bruises.

Agnes leaned a hip against the sink and cupped Josie's cheek. "How's her mama doing?"

Josie's eyes drifted to the suds in the sink, watching bubbles rise to the surface of the dishwater and pop. Kind of like her dreams. "Praying for a miracle that seems out of reach."

"Where's your faith, girl?"

"I think it's stored in a shoebox in my closet or some other place where I'd need a step stool to reach it." She attempted a smile, but the muscles in her cheeks refused to cooperate.

Agnes wrapped an arm around her shoulder and squeezed. "See, that's the great thing about faith—the more you need, the bigger it grows. That little ole mustard seed turns into a mighty tree. Takes some watering, though."

Did tears count?

Josie closed her eyes. Her daughter's face with the dark circles and blotchy cheeks swam behind her eyelids. *God, you work miracles. Please give one to Hannah.*

Agnes rinsed the rest of the dishes and stacked them to dry. "You need to get out of here and go home to that sweet child."

"I have a few more things to do. You go ahead. I can finish up here."

The timer dinged.

Agnes reached for the oven mitts. "I'll take care of these. You do what you gotta do, so we can both get out of here."

As Agnes removed the batch of cookies from the oven and transferred them to the cooling rack, Josie headed into the dining room to close out the register.

Her shoulders sagged as she stuffed the receipts and cash into the bank bag and tried not to let today's lack of customers discourage her. All businesses had slow days, right? She blamed it on the weather. Or at least she hoped that was it. She couldn't afford to close her doors like other small businesses in the area had done in recent months. She needed the insurance for Hannah's medical bills.

Shadows of the flames from the electric fireplace crawled up the ice-blue walls and reflected off the framed prints of European cafes. She flipped the switch. The flames flickered, then died out.

"Sugar Pie, I'm outta here." Agnes wrapped a designer scarf around her cinnamon-colored curls like an old Hollywood movie star. Long and leggy, the transplanted Texan had a heart the size of Dallas.

"Thanks for covering for me today, Agnes."

"Anytime. That's why you pay me the big bucks." She winked, blew Josie a kiss and then headed out the front door.

Rusted Christmas bells hanging from a tattered ribbon—drooping with age and faded from sunlight—jangled against the glass as Agnes pulled the door closed behind her. Leftover from the previous owners of the old Baker's Hardware. Josie considered replacing them with shiny, polished bells when she redid the place. But they added charm, character. They reminded Josie of what used to be.

Things were different now. A fresh start. New paint covered the scars, the imperfections.

The trendy coffee shop on the corner. A new beginning.

Her blends and fresh baked pastries whetted appetites more than a block away. Pride or ego didn't tell her that. Her bank balance suggested, for once in her life, Josie had made a right choice. Business would pick back up again. It had to.

She'd give it all up, every drop and crumb, to have her daughter healthy again.

Bells from the old stone church down the street rang out the seventh hour, each note reminding Josie she needed to get moving. Hannah needed her.

The front door rattled again, startling Josie from her thoughts. A quick glance at the clock showed she was five minutes late in closing and had forgotten to turn the sign.

A man stepped through the door, closing it behind him. Dressed in a brown bomber jacket, cream cable-knit sweater and khaki cargo pants, he looked as if he had stepped from the pages of an Eddie Bauer catalog. The only thing missing was a pair of Ray-Ban aviators.

"I'm sorry, but I'm just about to close." Josie headed for the door to flip the sign to CLOSED, but when the man turned and smiled, her footsteps stalled. "Nick. You c-came."

He rubbed his hands together. "Hope you don't mind a visit instead of a phone call. I have to admit seeing you at the university surprised me. It's been a long time."

She nodded, wishing her voice wasn't clogged in her throat like a spoonful of peanut butter.

His long legs ate up the distance between them in a few strides. He reached for her hands, held her at arm's length and gave her a once-over. "Wow, you look incredible." He glanced around. "Owning a coffeehouse agrees with you. Decided against being a travel journalist, huh? Dreams can change."

She pulled her hands away and clasped them behind her back. She couldn't afford to let his charm soften her heart. She had a responsibility to Hannah. "Motherhood has a way of doing that."

"You have a child? You and your husband must be very blessed. Congratulations."

She jerked back as if she had been slapped. "Congratulations? Seriously?"

"Did I say something wrong? I'm sorry. I just assumed…" He rubbed his earlobe and stared over her shoulder.

"You're acting like you have no clue." She moved to the nearest table, straightening the chairs and centering the votive candles.

Nick gripped the back of one of the chairs. "Should I have known? I haven't been back to Ridgefield since graduation. How long ago did you leave?"

"Couldn't shake the dust from your boots fast enough, could you?" She snatched a *Family Circle* magazine off the couch and dropped it in the large wicker basket next to the fireplace.

Nick leveled her with a direct look. "What's going on here, Josie? Let's try again. *It is* good to see you."

"Is it?" She glared at him, then headed behind the counter for a cloth and bottle of sanitizer.

Nick released the chair and crossed his arms over his chest. "What did I do to make you so angry?"

Josie spritzed sanitizer on the table. "You didn't call, Nick. Not once. Not even when…not even when she was born. You weren't there." She scrubbed at the coffee ring embossed on the table, then threw down the rag. No use. The scar remained.

"But we had broken up." He took a step toward her.

"What did you expect?"

Josie held up a hand, and he stopped. "I expected you to be responsible."

He held up his hands, palms to the ceiling. "Responsible for what? I'm so lost a GPS couldn't bring me back to the starting point."

She dropped onto the couch in front of the fireplace and massaged her forehead. "I needed you."

Nick rubbed his eyes with his thumb and forefinger. "Just tell me what you're talking about."

"Two years ago, *my* daughter, Hannah, was diagnosed with acute lymphocytic leukemia."

Nick sat on the matching chair across from her. "I'm so sorry."

"She went into remission, but the leukemia has come back. Now her doctor is recommending a bone marrow transplant. I've been tested, but I'm not a match. Testing her other parent is the most logical choice right now."

He shot her a puzzled look. "What does that have to do with me?"

Josie jumped to her feet and planted her fists on her hips. "Are you seriously this clueless, Professor? Choosing not to be a part of your daughter's life doesn't disqualify you from being her father."

Chapter Two

"Her what?" His words tripped their way up his throat. His heart hammered against his rib cage. "Did you just say I'm a...father?"

She had to be joking. One look at her crossed arms and jutted chin showed she told the truth. He stood and moved away from her, needing a little distance. Grabbing on to the mantel, he stared at the black pit where logs lay cold. Fake. Not real. Imitation. Just like him.

"My daughter is nine years old, Nick. She'll be ten in April. You're the one with the fancy degrees. Figure it out."

This could not be happening. There had to be some mistake. Wouldn't he have known? Or at least been told? He faced her again. "How do you know she's mine?"

"Because you're the only person I've been with. That night after my *nonna's* funeral when we..." She looked away, her words trailing off. A strand of hair slipped out of her clip and curled against her cheek.

A tucked away memory filtered through his head. After her grandmother's funeral, he had taken her for a drive down by the lake. He held her while she cried and kissed away her tears. He had known better, but in the heat of the moment, common sense fell away as quickly as their clothes. Regret coated his throat.

And now they had a child.

Pink tinged her cheeks. "I got pregnant. Hannah is your daughter, too."

"So you decided to wait until you needed something to tell me?"

Her head snapped up, her brown eyes the size of teacups. "Excuse me? Don't you dare act like this is news."

"How am I supposed to act? I'm hearing about this child for the first time." His words, laced with self-loathing, burned his tongue.

She jumped to her feet, nearly tripping over the coffee table, and poked him in the chest. "I called your mother and begged for your address, but she said it was best that I didn't hold you back."

A chill washed over him. He grabbed her wrist. "Wait a second. My mom knew you were pregnant?"

She pulled her hand free and backed away from him.

"Of course she did. When she refused to give me your address, she said she'd relay the message and let you decide. Actions really do speak louder than words, don't they?"

"She never told me." He scrubbed a hand over his face. *Mom, what have you done?*

"Yeah, right." She scoffed and rolled her eyes. "You couldn't wait to leave Ridgefield for your big shot college and put everything behind you, including me. Now you're blaming your mom for your lack of decency. I expected more from you, Nick. Funny how expectations end up being disappointments, too."

Nick fisted his hands to keep from shaking her. Did she seriously think he'd have walked out on her if he had known? Especially what she knew about his childhood?

"I swear I didn't know."

Her eyes narrowed. "I don't believe you."

"It's the truth."

Josie's shoulders sagged. She dropped on the couch, cradling her head in her hands. "Why wouldn't she tell you?"

Nick sighed and jammed his hands in his pockets. "I have no idea."

She pointed to the cordless phone on the counter. "Give her a call now and ask."

"I can't." Guilt gripped his vocal cords and twisted. He massaged his throat. Eight years. Still not long enough to forgive himself for destroying his family. "She's dead."

Her hand flew to her mouth. "I'm sorry. What happened? Wait. That's none of my business."

"Car accident." He didn't mention he was the one driving. He pushed ghosts of that night out of his thoughts and focused on the petite Italian beauty in front of him.

"So it's you and your brother now? Ross, right? How's he?"

"Yes, Ross. He's...fine." And he was. For the most part. He couldn't tell her about Ross. Not yet.

"I—I thought you knew about Hannah. I'm sorry this is such a shock." She reached up and touched his arm. "But she's your daughter, and she needs your help, Nick."

The pleading in her eyes cut him to the core. In the past ten minutes, his world had been turned upside down. He needed a minute to collect his thoughts.

Turning away, he swept his gaze over a rough-hewn bookcase decorated with ivy and tiny white lights. A stack of books lay on their sides next to a trio of chunky candlesticks in the corner. Cans of tea for sale lined the middle shelf. One of the labels on the tea can boasted an unforgettable experience. He didn't need to drink tea to have that. It had been handed to him the moment he walked through the door.

He remembered another door, a lifetime ago. The one his father walked out of when Nick was in first grade, leaving him with a sobbing mother and a screaming baby brother. Seeing his father throw that duffel bag in the back of the rusted pickup and barrel down the street had Nick racing after him, screaming his name and crying. He hadn't seen his dad since. He promised his mother and brother he'd never abandon his family.

But he had done just that to his daughter. He was no better than his father. A pain knifed his gut, threatening to drag the breath right out of him. He pressed a fist against his sternum.

"And then what, Josie?" His voice sounded hoarse to his own ears.

"What do you mean?" She sounded halfway across the room.

He turned and stared, drinking in the dark, loose curls escaping her clip and framing her face, the way her blue shirt and brown pants clung to her soft curves. With the dimmed overhead lighting casting shadows on her, she appeared no more than seventeen. The same age as when he got her pregnant. "What happens after I get tested?"

"Well, we wait to see if you're a match." She tugged on the hem of her shirt.

He took a step toward her. "No, I mean with Hannah and me. With you and me."

Her eyes flashed. "There is no you and me. You burned that bridge a long time ago."

He'd thought it was the best thing for them. Even after he started his freshman year, he'd thought of her often, had been so tempted to pick up the phone just to hear her voice, but he resisted. He'd had no right to lead her on.

Maybe that was why she hadn't tried a little harder to contact him. He glanced at her hand. No wedding ring. That didn't mean she wasn't in a relationship now. "There will always be a you and me. Now that I know about Hannah, I want to be a part of her life."

She shot him a "you've got to be kidding" look. "You don't even know her."

"Not by choice. Now that I have a chance, I'm not going to walk away." He was not going to be his father. He had to prove to Josie—somehow, some way—that he was in this for the long haul.

"I will not let you hurt her. She's been through so much already." Her voice shook. Her fingers trembled as she reached up and released the clip from her hair. It cascaded down her back like a waterfall.

"I promise you—I will never hurt her. I can put her on my insurance." He waved a hand toward the front of the store. "This is a great little place, but I can help you financially."

Josie's eyes narrowed. "I didn't ask for your money. I want only one thing—a blood test. Hannah's life depends on you."

He couldn't change the past, but he could make up for it. Starting now. She didn't have to do things alone again. He was here to help. If only he could get her to see that.

How could he prove he was committed to their daughter? His heart stuttered as a sudden thought crossed his mind. No, he couldn't. It was crazy. Before common sense could engage, he opened his mouth. "Marry me."

If he had suddenly sprouted a horn from the middle of his forehead, Josie wouldn't have been more shocked. She stared at him. "Excuse me?"

"You heard me." He stepped closer.

"No. No, I don't think I did." She swallowed and tried not to inhale the richness of his cologne. His closeness stirred feelings she'd stuffed away a long time ago. Feelings that got her into trouble.

"Josie——"

"Are you insane?" She stepped back, needing distance. "I asked you for a blood test, you idiot. Not for a marriage proposal. You're crazy."

He raised an eyebrow and leaned against a table, arms crossed over his chest. "I'm serious."

"So am I." She threw her hands in the air and muttered something in Italian that would've gotten her in trouble as a child. "Who in their right mind marries a guy off the street?"

"I'm not exactly a stranger."

She whirled around and searched his face for a hint of common sense. "To Hannah, you are. I haven't seen you in over ten years. I have no idea who you are anymore. A little girl's life is at stake here, and you're playing games." Funny how the Nick she knew back then was completely different than the man standing in front of her.

He watched her without saying a word. His jaw clenched. He was serious.

What a mess this was becoming. "Nick——"

Nick pushed away from the table and shoved his hands in his front pockets. "I missed out on nine years of my daughter's life. I'm not going to have some test done, give her another piece of me and disappear for the rest of her life. I have a responsibility now. I won't abandon my family."

"*Your* family? Where were you when she was teething? Where were you on the first day of kindergarten? Where were you when she spent the night throwing up after her first chemo treatment? We quit being yours the day Hannah was born, and you didn't show up."

"Not. My. Fault." His voice rose. "Maybe if you had faced me yourself, we wouldn't be here right now."

He blamed her? "I was seventeen, living at home, without a high school diploma, much less a job. You expected me to chase you across two states in the off chance you just might want to play house? I don't think so." Her chest heaved.

She grabbed the back of the couch and dug her fingers into the fabric. She drew in a deep breath and blew it out slowly before facing him again. Feeling a tiny bit calmer, she turned back to him. "When you didn't show up after I called your mother, I wrote you out of our lives. But now I'll do whatever it takes to save Hannah's life. Even if it means dealing with you again."

Nick closed the distance between them in two strides and placed both hands on her shoulders. "If I had known about Hannah from day one, I would have been there. I would have given it all up to raise her with you." Nick's gaze pierced her soul. "That option was taken from me. I can't make up the past, but I will be a part of her life—with or without your consent."

Josie's heart raced. Was he threatening her? She pulled his hands off her shoulders, squeezed his fingers and softened her tone. "Look, I respect your wanting to be a part of her life, but that doesn't mean we have to get married. Come on, Nick, get real. Who does that? Besides, how could I marry someone I can't even be sure is going to stick around?" She had plenty of experience with people claiming to love her and then leaving.

"When can I see her?"

What if she didn't let him see her? Would he refuse to get tested? She couldn't risk it. Josie let go of his hands and glanced at the large clock above the fireplace. She was so late. Would Hannah still be awake? How would she even begin to explain Nick to her? Maybe the best way would be to have Hannah meet Nick, explain why he was there and then let the two of them get to know each other with her nearby. "Let me lock up, and we can head to my house now."

"She's home alone?"

The accusation in his voice scored a direct hit. Did he think she was that irresponsible?

"No, Nonno—my grandfather—lives with us. Usually I only work until noon, but worked this afternoon to catch up from being away this morning."

"Does she know about me?" The uncertainty in his voice nearly melted her anger.

She sighed and then shook her head. "Not really. I mean, I haven't kept you a huge secret or anything, but she knows you as an ex-high school boyfriend. She's seen yearbook pictures. That's about it."

"And my mom never contacted you?"

"Not once."

"I'm sorry."

She lifted a shoulder. "Sorry can't erase the last ten years."

"Regardless of what you think of me, if I had known, I wouldn't have just left you to face everything alone."

"Well, we can't exactly turn back time, can we? So I guess we'll never know. You have a choice now. Just don't screw it up."

Josie flicked off the dining room lights, leaving on a row above the front counter edged against the large storefront window. "I'm going through the kitchen and out the back door. I'll meet you out front and then you can follow me home."

"Fine."

As soon as he headed outside, Josie flipped the deadbolt into place, hurried through the kitchen, grabbed her purse off her desk and snatched her coat off the chair. She slammed through the back door.

Her fingers shook so badly that she dropped her keys in the snow slumped against the back of the building. She fished them out with bare fingers and leaned against the door, staring at the night sky as she pulled in large gulps of frosty air. She locked the door and trudged through the snow to her car.

Five minutes later, Josie pulled onto Songbird Lane and into her driveway with Nick's headlights in her rearview mirror.

"You can do this. For Hannah." Taking a deep breath, she clenched the steering wheel. With a final sigh, she grabbed her purse off the passenger seat and climbed out, slamming the door behind her.

Nick's shoulders hunched close to his ears as he blew into his bare hands. "Feels like January instead of March."

They were going to discuss the weather? Seriously?

His eyes shifted to her house, his lips turning upward. "It's something out of a Disney movie."

Shrubs of various shapes and sizes clustered against the front and around the sides of the stone cottage. Brittle limbs sighed over a chipped picket fence as if they carried the weight of winter. Cleared cobblestones meandered in a haphazard path to the red front door.

"Wait until you see the fairy door knocker. Hannah fell in love with it when we moved here." Maybe small talk would help her forget about the pain eroding her heart. Doubtful.

"When was that?"

"Once I graduated from college—about five years ago

or so." Josie shoved her hands in her pockets and started up the walk. "She was in her Disney princesses phase."

She opened the door, stepped inside then moved out of the way so he could enter. A small candlestick lamp on the semicircle foyer table by the front door lit the entryway. Shadows stretched across the wood floor that led into the living room. Josie dropped her purse on the table, shrugged off her coat and hung it in an open closet. She didn't offer to take Nick's. He wouldn't be staying long.

She stepped into the bathroom around the corner from the front door and washed her hands. Returning to the hall, she nodded toward the bathroom. "Please wash your hands. We have to be really careful about germs."

Without saying a word, Nick moved past her and did as she asked. She marched into the large living room without checking to see if he followed.

She passed by the taupe leather couch with its aqua-and-chocolate pillows and crocheted afghan and crossed to the matching recliner to kiss her grandfather's cheek. He rested with his eyes closed and a suspense novel open on his chest. The soft glow of the tall candlestick lamp behind his chair bathed his face, filling in the lines and wrinkles of life's experiences. "*Nonno,* I'm home."

Her grandfather started, adjusting his glasses on his nose. "*Cara, mi avete spaventato.* You startled me." His eyes shifted over her shoulder.

"So sorry. I have a guest." She waved her hand toward Nick.

"A guest, you say." Her grandfather lowered his footrest and eased himself out of the chair. He straightened his brown knitted vest over his blue plaid shirt.

Josie placed a hand on her grandfather's shoulder. "*Nonno,* meet Nick Brennan."

"Nick, this is my *nonno*, I mean my grandfather, Vincenzo Peretti."

"A pleasure, sir." Nick extended a hand.

"Nick." *Nonno's* voice trailed off and his lips thinned as his eyes narrowed. "Are you...?" He shot a look at Josie. She nodded, biting the inside of her lip. "Yes, he's Hannah's father."

Nonno pulled his shoulders back, stepped toward Nick and pointed a finger at him. "You have some nerve. What kind of man puts an innocent girl in a family way and then disappears?"

Josie placed a hand on his chest. "*Nonno*, not now." Nick held up a hand. "Sir, you have every right to be angry. I'm sure I would be, too, in your place. In my defense, I didn't know."

"Didn't know? Didn't know? Why, that's preposterous. I remember—"

"*Nonno*, we'll talk later." She linked her arm through his and pressed a kiss to his temple.

Nonno glared at Nick. Josie had to give him credit for not backing down. Her grandfather was the first to break eye contact. Muttering in Italian, he returned to his recliner and picked up his book, pretending to read.

Josie removed the novel from his hands, turned it right side up and smiled. "*Ti amo.*"

"*Ti amo, cara.*"

She swallowed a lump in her throat. "Where's Hannah?"

"She's asleep. I checked on her about half an hour ago."

"*Grazie.*"

Josie motioned for Nick to follow her and headed up the stairs separating the living room from the dining room. Putting her finger to her lips, Josie pushed her daughter's bedroom door open and tiptoed to Hannah's bed where she lay curled in a ball, one arm clutching Duck, her stuffed purple alligator that had seen better days.

Josie looked over her shoulder to where Nick stood rooted to the threshold. His eyes didn't waver from the bed. His brows furrowed and then a look she couldn't interpret crossed over his face.

"What's wrong?" Josie's heart fluttered. He was probably in shock about Hannah's baldness.

"She's beautiful."

Chapter Three

After Nick left, Josie managed to fall asleep for about three hours before her alarm should have gone off. Except she had forgotten to set her alarm.

Josie arrived at Cuppa Josie's late and found the back door frozen shut again. She and Hannah traipsed around to the front door.

The wind whipped the beige-and-blue-striped canopy over the smoky glass door with the steaming cup etched in white.

Josie balanced a box of tulips in order to jiggle the key in the ancient front door lock, making a mental note to salt the sidewalk.

Hannah's narrow shoulders hunched against the blustery weather. "Hurry up, Mom. It's so cold."

"Really? And here I was taking my time so I could work on my tan." Josie closed her eyes, flung out her free arm and raised her face to the sky.

"Ha. Ha. Very funny." The biting air rouged Hannah's cheeks and the tip of her upturned nose, adding a blush of color to her skin.

"Hold these, please." Josie handed the box of tulips to Hannah, tugged her daughter's hat down over her forehead and then rewrapped the purple-and-white-striped scarf around her neck.

"Need a hand?"

She turned to see Nick shutting the door to a shiny black Ford Ranger and stepping onto the sidewalk.

What was he doing here? They weren't supposed to meet until later. She hadn't talked to Hannah yet.

She gave him a tight smile and moved Hannah in front of her. "Thanks, but I got it."

Come on, Lord, cut a girl a break here.

The hairs on the back of her neck bristled. Was he still there? Watching them? She snuck a peek over her shoulder.

Blowing into cupped hands, he stood about four feet behind them, eyes focused on them.

Did he have to watch her every move?

The key turned. Josie's exhaled breath puffed against the glass as she opened the door.

Josie guided Hannah inside and pushed the door closed, but Nick shot forward and grabbed the handle. "Is it too early to come in?"

Josie darted a look between Hannah and him. Hannah gave her a curious look.

"If it makes you uncomfortable, I can wait in my truck." He thrust a thumb over his shoulder toward the street. He took a step back.

She paused. "No, don't do that. Come in. I'll have the coffee going in a few minutes." She flicked on the interior light and flipped the CLOSED sign to OPEN.

She handed him the *Shelby Lake Gazette* and gestured toward the high-backed stools hugging the counter. "Grab a chair. Coffee will be ready shortly."

With no time for introductions, she and Hannah wove their way around the square tables, shed their coats in her office and then washed their hands. Hannah traded her winter hat for a pink checked newsboy cap and tugged it sideways on her head. She pulled her iPod and a book from her backpack. Grabbing a banana out of the hanging basket near the sink, she perched on a stool next to the stainless-steel counter where Josie rolled out her piecrusts.

Within minutes of starting the coffee, the mingling scents of the different blends breathed life into Josie and flowed through her as necessarily as her own blood. Even though she couldn't drink coffee, she craved the smell.

The front door jangled.

Oh, no. Not yet. She wasn't ready for customers—the coffee hadn't finished brewing. The pastry case wore empty shelves. The candles hadn't been lit. The fireplace lay cold.

Why, oh, why hadn't she set her cell phone to go off, too?

Agnes pushed through the swinging kitchen door. "Sugar Pie, so sorry I'm late. I had no electricity and had to go to Mama's to dry my hair." She hung up her coat and fluffed snowflakes off her curls. "Back door stuck again? I nearly slid on my tush coming around to the front."

Josie pointed to Agnes's feet. "Wear something a little more sensible than those stiletto boots."

Agnes struck a model pose. "But they make my legs look long and lean. Never know when Mr. Right is going to come along."

"Didn't you get your fill of marriage after your ex left you for that perky pop star wannabe?" Josie twisted her hair and clipped it in a messy updo, pulling down a few loose curls to frame her face.

Agnes made a face. "What's up with Mr. Yummy at the counter out there? Picking up strays again?"

Josie glanced at Hannah and gave Agnes a slight shake of her head.

Agnes's eyebrows notched into a V and then her eyes widened as her mouth puckered into an O.

Josie nodded, appreciating her friend's understanding. "At least we baked last night. Mind filling the pastry case while I get the store ready?"

"Not at all." Agnes changed her boots into more sensible shoes, then washed and dried her hands. She dropped a kiss on Hannah's temple, leaving behind a lipstick imprint. "How are you, darlin'?"

Hannah smiled and fingered one of Agnes's large gold hoops. "Hey, Aggie. Love your earrings. *Someday* I'll be allowed to get my ears pierced."

Josie pressed the back of her hand against her forehead and sagged against the counter. "Oh, the perils of being a kid."

Hannah shot her a look that said she was not amused. Josie shrugged and bit the inside of her lip.

"Sugar Pie, you have the rest of your life to play grown-up. Don't you be rushing anything now. You hear me?" Agnes grabbed two blue aprons and tossed one to Josie. "And don't be giving your mama a big to-do about it. She's doing right by making you wait."

"Seriously, I just don't see what the big deal is about getting my ears pierced."

Josie tied the apron around her waist and smoothed the front. "The big deal is we agreed you could get them done when you turn ten. Keep griping about it and I'll make you wait until you're sixteen."

Hannah's eyes widened. "You wouldn't."

"Try me." Josie raised an eyebrow at her daughter.

"So not fair. Especially for a sick kid." Hannah returned to her book.

Josie tugged on one of the earbuds to snag her daughter's attention. "Don't play that card with me, kiddo. I mean it."

Lakeside Family

"Sorry." Hannah leaned against Josie.

Josie swallowed the apple-size lump in her throat. Her eyes connected with Agnes's, which seemed overly bright.

Less than ten minutes later, Josie carried full pots of today's special blends—Almond Toffee Crunch and Hazelnut Cream—and placed them on the coffee bar to the left of the register. She turned to head back into the kitchen for the regular and decaf, but paused and cocked her head.

What was that scraping sound?

She threaded her way around the tables to the front window. Outside the shop, Nick had cleared the ice. And now he tossed handfuls of ice melter on the sidewalk.

With trying to get the shop ready, she had forgotten about the sidewalks. Something deep shimmied to the surface, filling her with warmth at his thoughtfulness.

As a teenager, he had always been willing to lend a hand.

He looked up and lifted his hand in greeting.

He still had a really great smile. Not that she paid attention to him specifically or anything. Working with the public, a girl noticed these things.

She turned away, and nearly tripped over a chair. A quick peek over her shoulder showed he had indeed seen her klutzy move. His grin sent heat across her cheeks.

Way to go, Josie.

A few minutes later, the door opened. Nick returned the bucket of ice melter and shovel behind the front door where he had found them.

Josie plated a chocolate chip muffin and warmed it in the microwave. She grabbed a stout-bellied glass mug off the shelf behind the register and then carried them to the front counter where Nick had shrugged out of his bomber jacket. Water droplets dampened his hair. The tips of his ears were reddened from the cold. Dressed in a light blue

T-shirt, an unbuttoned blue-and-white-striped dress shirt, loose fitting jeans and a pair of beat-up Converses on his feet, he looked more like a college student than a professor.

She set the mug on the counter and pointed to the coffee bar, hating the way her fingers trembled. She clenched them into fists, hoping he didn't notice. "Help yourself to coffee. Today's specials are Almond Toffee Crunch and Hazelnut Cream."

"Thanks." He smiled and pulled his wallet out of his back pocket.

Josie shook her head. "On the house. You didn't need to clean my walk."

He turned sideways, resting one elbow on the back of the chair and another on the spread newspaper. "Your friend almost slipped. And you were busy."

"I would've gotten to it." She winced at the defensive tone in her voice.

He held up a hand. "Hey, that wasn't a criticism."

"Sorry. Thanks." She shut her mouth before finishing off a course of foot-in-mouth. She moved to the fireplace and flipped the switch. Flames came to life and tangoed across the fake logs. If she closed her eyes, she could pretend to hear crackles and smell burning pine.

Nick slid off the stool and wrapped long fingers around the mug. "Wasn't a problem. Really."

For him, maybe. He wasn't the irresponsible one who couldn't even get out of bed on time.

"Do you have time for coffee? To talk?"

She glanced at the clock. "Not now. Besides, I don't drink coffee."

He headed to the coffee bar and filled his mug. "What kind of barista owns a coffeehouse, but doesn't drink coffee?"

She dashed behind the counter and grabbed the candle lighter. "The kind who's allergic to caffeine."

"Then why a coffeehouse?"

"Coffee and food bring people together." She lit the votive candles nestled in a bed of coffee beans on each table.

He nodded toward the word wall next to the fireplace. "What's this? Saw it when I came in."

She shrugged. Would he think she was silly? Did she care? "A community word wall. Each month I put up miscellaneous words and challenge customers to create something unique. At the end of the month, they're voted on and the winner receives a free drink."

"Great way to inspire people to write."

Spoken like a true English professor.

Nick moved past her to get his coffee.

She stuck the candle lighter in her front pocket and grabbed the box of tulips still on the edge of the counter. She replaced the red-and-pink Valentine arrangements on the window counter and near the cash register with the potted tulips.

The front door jangled. Two women and a man in business attire entered, brushing snowflakes off the shoulders of their overcoats. Within minutes, a steady stream of customers filed through the café, keeping her busy behind the counter. The whirring of the espresso machine competed with the rustling of the morning newspapers, cell phone ring tones and chatter.

Emmett Browne, one of her loyal customers and true genius with a camera, banged on the counter with his hand-carved cane. "Josie, where's the paper? I come in here every morning, sit in the same spot to do the morning crossword, and today of all days, you open late and the paper is missing. What is this world coming to?" His salt-

and-pepper eyebrows knitted together. His sausage fingers gripped the curve of his cane. Tufts of white hair sprouted beneath his tweed fedora.

Josie smiled and turned to reach for a glass mug. She set it on the counter in front of him. "Good morning to you, too, Emmett. The usual?"

"Don't I always have the usual? Did you forget already? What's so hard about a black coffee and a banana nut muffin? And don't slip me any of that bran malarkey. I can tell the difference, you know." He pulled out two dollar bills and a handful of change. He laid the bills on the counter and counted out sixty-eight cents and then tossed two quarters in the tip jar.

"Of course not. One of the other customers is reading the paper. As soon as he's finished, you can do your crossword."

He glowered at her. "And what am I supposed to do in the meantime? What kind of establishment gives out one paper?"

"Try being patient. Would you like me to go buy you another paper?" She pointed to the yellow paper box outside her shop.

"Harrumph. Now, that would be a waste of money, wouldn't it?" He hobbled over to one of the armchairs near the fireplace and eased his body onto the cushion. Dropping his hat on the side table, he laid his cane on the floor and glared at Nick.

Agnes opened the small fridge under the espresso machine for the milk. "Why do you put up with that codger's attitude?"

"He's lonely and all bark but no bite. If griping at me makes him happy, I can turn the other cheek. Today's a rough day for him." Josie warmed a banana nut muffin and slipped a blueberry one into a small paper bag. She carried both to Emmett, who sat tapping his pen against the arm of the chair.

"Here's your muffin. And a little something for later." She handed him the white bag.

He eyed the bag. "What is it?"

"A blueberry muffin."

His shoulders slumped. "Elsie's favorite."

She crouched beside him and patted his hand. "Rough day, huh?"

"Forty-eight years." He traced the plain gold band embedded in his finger while gazing into the fire. "She was my everything. I miss her."

She squeezed his hand, feeling his pain. "I know."

He pressed his lips against her knuckles. "Thanks for the extra muffin."

"Anything for you, Emmett." Josie patted his cheek.

The phone rang, but Agnes snagged it. She covered the phone with her hand. "Josie, Billy Lynn's on the phone asking about his doughnut order?"

Josie left Emmett and hurried to the counter. "Doughnut order?"

The words were no sooner out of her mouth when she spotted the pink sticky note reminding her about the six dozen doughnuts requested by the fire department. That was the baking thing she was forgetting. She sighed and resisted the urge to bang her head against the pastry case. If she hadn't overslept, the doughnuts would be ready and waiting by now.

She reached for the phone. "Hey, Billy. This is Josie. I'm running behind today. When's the latest I can get them to you?"

"Would noon be pushing it?"

Eyeing the clock, she did a mental calculation. "No, I can handle that. Again, I'm sorry."

"Bring me a cup of that Almond Toffee Crunch coffee and I'll forgive you, Dollface."

"I'll bring you a whole pot."

"Josie!" The alarm in Agnes's voice sent ice through Josie's veins.

Hannah!

"Billy, I gotta go." She sprinted through the swinging kitchen door. The kitchen was empty. "Agnes? Hannah? Where are you?"

"The storeroom. Hurry your fanny in here."

Josie hurried past her office to the storeroom near the back door. Her nose wrinkled against a musty, sulfur smell. Gross.

She rounded the corner to find Agnes and Hannah staring at the ceiling. She followed their gazes. Her stomach plummeted to her toes. She groaned and slumped against the doorjamb. "Oh, no! Oh, please no. Not now. Not this." Josie squeezed her eyes shut, counted to ten in Italian—*uno, due, tre, quattro, cinque, sei, sette, otto, nove, dieci*—and then opened her eyes, praying what she saw had been a mistake. Or a trick of the eyes.

No such luck.

A section of the ceiling in the storeroom hung down like an escape hatch. Soaked drywall, exposed beams and floor joists and dripping insulation drooped from the damaged area. Water droplets beaded along old iron plumbing pipes. Blackened puckers stretched along the seams in the upstairs apartment's wooden floor.

The drain in the floor gurgled as dripping water spiraled into the circular grate. Most of her baking supplies had been stored in airtight plastic containers, so at least they were spared. But looking at the gaping ceiling again, she could almost see the money flowing out of her bank account. *Okay, God, a cork would be nice. So much for paying this month's mortgage on time.*

Nick grabbed his cell phone and checked the time. He hadn't seen Josie in a while. Had she forgotten they planned to talk at 8:30, which was ten minutes ago? Maybe she was ticked because he had shown up so early, but hey, a guy can count the ceiling tiles in his hotel room only so long. Nothing good on the tube this early in the morning, anyway, so he headed in to get a cup of coffee. Besides, he had an idea to discuss with her about Hannah.

Seeing Hannah with her nearly caused his legs to give out. The child looked more like she was six or seven than close to ten. Josie didn't seem thrilled to see him, but what was he expecting? A hero's welcome? A loving hug? Not going to happen. Especially since she thought he had bailed all those years ago.

"Finished with that plate, Sugar Pie?"

Nick looked up from scanning the Knicks score to find the same redhead who nearly slipped on the icy walk standing next to him. He smiled. "Yes, thanks."

She grabbed the plate and sashayed back to the kitchen. No other way to describe her walk.

Some old guy kept giving him the evil eye. He had been minding his own business, reading the paper. Giving a mental shrug, he returned to the sports section to finish reading the highlights of last night's game. Or at least pretend to.

About half an hour ago, Hannah came out of the kitchen and settled at a corner table with her nose in a book. She didn't take her eyes off the page, but Nick couldn't keep his eyes off his daughter. The way she bit her lip reminded him of Josie. If Hannah had hair, would she twirl a curl around her finger the way her mother did?

Maybe he could go over and talk to her.

That would send Josie through the roof. Besides, he didn't want to risk upsetting the child. He had to do something, though. Sitting here was driving him nuts. He folded the newspaper, set it on the counter and moved off the stool to head for the kitchen. If she didn't come to him, he'd go to her.

The old man who had been giving him the evil eye appeared at his side. "Mind if someone else takes a gander at the paper?"

"Have at it." Nick pushed it toward him.

The man shuffled through the pages until he found what he had been looking for. "Hey, you did the crossword! In pen. I don't believe it."

"Is that a problem?"

"I do the crossword. Every morning at 7:15, I get a coffee, a banana nut muffin and then do the crossword until it's time to visit my son."

"I'm sorry, sir. I'll head outside and buy you a new paper." Nick grabbed his coat.

"Don't bother. No time now. The morning's been disrupted enough." The man shoved the paper back onto the counter.

Out of the corner of his eye, he saw Josie come from the kitchen. He put a hand on the man's shoulder. "I am sorry. I promise not to touch the crossword again. Now, if you'll excuse me."

He strode to the counter to catch her before she pulled another disappearing act. She wasn't hiding because of him, was she?

She spun away from the register and pushed open the swinging door, but Nick caught her elbow. She whirled around to face him.

"Nick."

"We were supposed to talk. Remember?"

She shot a glance at the clock and then sighed. "Oh, that's right. I'm so sorry. It's been a crazy morning. Listen, I'm not trying to blow you off or anything, but I have a major water leak to deal with, a doughnut order to rush and then I have to take Hannah to the doctor at two. Can we talk later?"

"Where's her doctor?"

"A couple of blocks from here. Dr. Kym."

"I have an appointment at 11:30, but I could meet you at the doctor afterward."

"That's not necessary." She cast a glance toward Hannah and then edged toward the still-open kitchen door.

Nick gave her a pointed look. "She's my daughter, too. Remember? I need to know what's going on with her."

She grabbed his hand and pulled him into the kitchen. "I haven't had time to tell Hannah about you. You can't just show up as some random guy. And I'm not going to introduce you in the doctor's office. You're bound to be a shock to her."

As much as he hated to admit it, Josie made sense. He remembered last night's stunned feeling when he learned he had a daughter. How would the kid feel once she learned dear old dad finally showed up? "All right, then. How about if the three of us go to dinner?"

"Can't." Josie picked up a rag and wiped crumbs off the counter.

Nick crossed his arms and leaned against the doorjamb. "You want me to get tested, but you don't want me to be a part of her life?"

With her back to him, she rinsed the dishcloth in the sink. "No, it's not that at all. My family is coming to dinner tonight. Hannah can't be around a lot of people right now with her immune system being so weak. I risked her health by bringing her into the shop this morning, but I had no choice."

"What happened?"

She turned around. "I overslept. My grandfather had an appointment today and won't be home until dinner. My stepsister is coming to pick up Hannah. Because of the water leak, I don't want her in the kitchen." She sighed and rubbed her forehead. "It's been one disaster after another."

"Sounds like you need a vacation."

"Yeah, well, that's not going to happen." Her eyes filled with a sadness that tugged at his heart.

He wanted to pull her into his arms and tell her everything was going to be okay, but touching her was the last thing she wanted. Plus, he didn't believe in giving false hope or meaningless platitudes because he didn't know if everything was going to work out. From his past experience he knew how life had a way of dishing out trash no one deserved.

Chapter Four

If Josie had a quarter for every "if only" that popped into her brain, she'd be able to pay off the rest of Hannah's medical bills and head south to their dream beach house on the Gulf Coast of Florida.

She stared through the gaping hole in the bathroom floor in the upstairs apartment down to her shop. Like the one in her pocket.

Was this how Alice felt when she peered down the rabbit hole?

Okay, maybe not quite, but Josie had the sensation of falling into a very deep well—one not lined with Ben Franklins.

Footprints had been tracked through the plaster dust and muddied the water-stained brown tile in the storeroom. The same dust coated the metal storage racks and plastic totes. Swollen ceiling tiles lay tossed on the floor.

All because of a tiny...what did Harv call that little doohickey thing? She tried, she really did, to listen as her contractor explained the plumbing problem in lingo she could understand. He was the expert, after all. But her thoughts kept returning to the cost to fix the mess. Not to mention the stench pickled her brain.

If only she hadn't forgotten to call Harv to fix that leaky toilet when her previous tenant had mentioned it. But once Hannah's leukemia returned, everything else dropped on her priority list. If only… No, she wasn't going there. She didn't have time for pity parties. Especially when Hannah had it so much worse.

"Josie, did you hear what I said?"

Josie swung her gaze to Harv, who stood next to Ian James, her insurance man. Both men wore grim expressions that did little to soothe the ache in her stomach.

"I'm sorry, Harv. I disappeared down a rabbit hole."

"Climb back out, Alice. We have some figures to discuss." The creases around his eyes deepened as he winked at her. He tugged his John Deere baseball hat out of his back pocket and plopped it on top of his balding head.

Josie jerked her head toward the door. "Let's go downstairs. I'll get you guys some coffee."

Ian held the door for them. "Say, Josie. Is Agnes working?"

As Josie passed by him, she took in his black suit, white creaseless shirt, and trimmed hair. "Yes, Ian, but roll up your tongue. She doesn't need another man in her life right now."

"When did you become her mother?" he muttered, following her down the stairs.

"After I cleaned up the train wreck of her marriage. You saw what that jerk did to her." Josie opened the door and stepped onto the sidewalk. A late-winter breeze whisked across her cheeks.

"Josie, chill. I'm not going to cheat on her. I just want to take her to dinner."

Entering the coffee shop, Josie sniffed the scent of freshly baked blueberry cobbler. Her stomach growled. "Everyone's charming on the first date, aren't they?"

"When did you become so cynical?" He smoothed a hand over his hair.

Josie opened her mouth and then shut it. No need to yank those skeletons from her closet. Shelby Lake was her fresh start.

She gentled her voice and placed a hand on his arm. "Listen, Ian, you're a great guy, but take it slow, okay? Agnes looks like she has it all together, but her heart is pieced together with Scotch Tape."

Ian pocketed his Clark Kent glasses and stared over her shoulder a minute. Then he pulled his gaze back to meet hers. He touched the tip of her nose. "Are you sure you're still talking about Agnes?"

"Positive. Find a table. I need to pull cobbler out of the oven." Before he had a chance to protest, Josie whirled away from him.

Crazy talk.

Her heart was just fine, thank you very much.

Besides, she and Agnes looked out for each other. That's what friends did.

She pushed through the kitchen door and knocked heads with Agnes. So much for looking out for her.

"Sugar Pie, where's the fire?" Agnes rubbed the right side of her forehead.

Josie sniffed back sudden tears as she scrunched her throbbing eye closed. "Sorry, Aggie. I didn't see you."

Agnes primped her curls. "And here, I thought I made my hair extra high this morning. Figured you could've seen it through the window."

"Yeah, if I was looking for Texas-size hair."

"How'd it go upstairs?"

"Ugh." Josie gloved her hands with pink pig oven mitts and pulled open the oven door. Heat pressed against her face and neck. She pulled out a bubbling blueberry cobbler and set it on top of the stove.

"That good, huh?"

Josie slapped the mitts next to the dessert, crossed her arms and leaned one hip against the counter. "Am I a terrible person who deserves all of this grief? Doesn't seem fair."

"Life doesn't play fair, Sugar Pie. This ain't about you, so don't go taking this on yourself. You're doing the best you can with what you've got."

"If I had the toilet fixed when Beatrice mentioned it, we wouldn't be in this mess. A lousy two-dollar part would've saved me thousands. What sort of responsible business owner am I?"

Agnes grabbed Josie's arms and squeezed gently. "The kind who is trying to do everything and be everything to everyone. Cut yourself some slack."

"If only—"

"No 'if onlys' about it. You could waste forever on shoulda woulda coulda. Yesterday Is all gone, thank you. Instead, focus on what you're going to do now to fix it. That's what matters. None of us expected this to happen."

Ian poked in his head in the kitchen. "Josie, Harv had a call and left. He said he'll stop back in later, but he left an estimate. And I need to head back to the office."

"I'm coming now." With Agnes on her heels, Josie followed him to the dining room table where Ian had his computer tablet and a yellow legal pad spread out.

Ian handed her an invoice. "This is Harv's estimate. He'll go over it with you later."

Josie's eyes widened at the number of zeroes to the left of the decimal point. She glanced at Agnes and Ian. "Twenty thousand? Seriously?"

Ian guided her to the chair and forced her to sit. He

took one beside her. "Don't worry, Josie. The insurance should cover it."

"Should?" Her voice squeaked. "It *has* to."

"Normally, yes, but in cases of neglect, things get a little dicey."

She gripped the edge of the paper. "Do you know how many cancer treatments twenty thousand will buy?" Not to mention, it could go a long way toward her growing pile of co-pays and medical bills. She couldn't afford to waste it on a stupid toilet problem.

Agnes set a steaming cup of tea in front of Josie. "Drink, Sugar Pie."

She cupped her hands around the mug, breathed in herbal mint and blinked back tears. "I can't afford this, Aggie. I could sell the shop, but then I'll lose Hannah's insurance."

Agnes pulled out a chair and sat opposite of Ian, sandwiching his hands between her own. "Ian James, you know as well as I do that Josie has been spending every possible minute with her daughter, taking her to the doctor and chemo treatments and keeping this place running."

"Of course, Agnes." The tips of his ears turned crimson. "Don't seem to me that it's neglect if she simply hasn't had time to attend to it. Why, that's just silly. Shame on you for making this poor girl cry. As if she doesn't have enough to worry about already. Now you be a good insurance man and file the paperwork so Josie doesn't have to worry her pretty little head about this anymore." She patted his cheek as if he were a six-year-old child being scolded for eating cookies before dinner.

Agnes stood and slid her hand under Josie's elbow, guiding her to stand. "Come along, Josie. Ian will take care of everything. Won't you, darlin'?"

Slack-jawed, Josie stared at her friend and then slid a

glance at Ian. The poor man was so smitten by Agnes—and no, she didn't blame him—he'd probably don a chicken suit and cluck if requested.

Pushing to his feet, Ian cleared his throat and ran a hand over his slicked-back hair. "Don't you worry about a thing, Josie. I'll make sure everything is taken care of. I'll call Harv and deal with him myself. Agnes is right. You have more important things to worry about."

Agnes rounded the table and showered him with a honey-laden smile. She brushed invisible lint off his jacket and straightened his narrow pinstriped tie. "You are a good, good man, Ian James. You and I both know Josie isn't neglectful. Forgetful, maybe, but can you blame the poor dear? Her mind is wrapped around her calendar and her daughter's health." Agnes spun on her toes and sashayed her size six Texas dynamo behind the counter to wait on a customer.

Ian fumbled to put his notepad and computer tablet in his hard-sided briefcase. He removed his glasses from his pocket and set them on his nose without taking his eyes off Agnes. "She's a firecracker, isn't she?"

Josie glanced over her at her friend and grinned. "That's one word for it."

Ian gave Josie's shoulder a squeeze and then ambled out the door, whistling.

Josie straightened the chairs and grabbed her cooling cup of tea. She set it on the counter by the espresso machine and applauded quietly. "That, my friend, deserved an Oscar."

Agnes looked up from the latte she was making. "Whatever do you mean?"

"That man is so sweet on you, he'd do anything you asked."

"All of this coffee has marinated your brain. You're imagining things."

"I didn't imagine that hole in the floor. I just hope the insurance will cover it."

"Ian will come through for you, Sugar Pie. And so will God. Just you wait and see."

Nick stood on the sidewalk in front of the white clapboard house with red shutters and checked the house number against the scribbles on his paper. It looked more like someone's home than a place for adults with special needs.

Before Josie whirled back into his life yesterday, Nick received a call from Miss Patty, his brother's group home caregiver, giving him a month to find a new place for Ross. Her son-in-law received orders to Okinawa, and Patty was moving to Virginia to be with her pregnant daughter. At least she gave him a place to check out—Jacob House, owned by her cousin Mae and her husband, Walt.

He needed to do this. For Ross.

His brother was going to lose it when moving day arrived. And being even farther from Linwood Park wasn't going to help with Nick's commute. Maybe he should just cancel the appointment.

Not an option. Patty was still moving, and Nick couldn't care for Ross by himself.

Exposed branches scratched at the multipaned dormer windows. He strode up the cleared sidewalk, making a mental note of the wheelchair ramp off to the side and covered with nonskid surfacing. Snow melted like leftover frosting over low evergreens hugging the rails of the wraparound porch. A black mailbox with a red cardinal painted on the front hung next to the door.

The wide front porch with the gray planked floor, padded wooden rockers and swaying porch swing made

Nick think of summer evenings shooting the breeze with neighbors or enjoying a quiet evening with the family while swigging iced tea from Mason jars.

The curtains in the window moved, and a pale face pressed to the glass stared at him. Nick lifted a hand. The face disappeared, leaving behind a smudge on the pane.

He wiped his feet on a bristled welcome mat and rang the doorbell, hearing the gongs echo throughout the interior. No turning back now.

The door opened, revealing a man with graying hair and wearing faded jeans and an Ohio State sweatshirt. A wide smile erased the drill instructor sternness from his forehead. "Good morning. You must be Nick. I'm Walt Hoffman." He held out a hand.

Nick shook it. "Nick Brennan."

"We spoke on the phone. Welcome to Jacob House. Come in and meet everyone." He stepped aside for Nick to enter.

The aroma of freshly baked bread reminded him of Josie's place. His mouth watered.

A woman with dark hair pulled into a ponytail and dressed in a denim jumper and white tennis shoes came out of the living room. "Good morning. You must be Nick. I'm Jane Vogt, one of the staffers. Let me take your coat."

"Nice to meet you, ma'am." He shook her hand and then shrugged off his jacket to hand to her. Over Jane's shoulder, three men stood in the living room doorway, whispering to each other.

Jane turned and laid her hand on the shoulder of one man with neatly combed red hair and wire-rimmed glasses. His almond-shaped eyes stared at Nick as his tongue protruded slightly from his mouth. He wore a green-and-yellow bowling shirt with Ernie stitched on the left pocket and hugged a Cabbage Patch-style doll dressed the same way, glasses and all. "Ernie, this is Nick Brennan. Nick, Ernie is one of our residents at Jacob House."

"Nice to meet you, Ernie." Nick held out his hand.

"Nice to meet you, too." Ernie spoke with a slight lisp as he reached for Nick's hand. He thrust the doll at Nick. "This is Frederick."

Nick shook Frederick's hand. "Nice to meet you, Frederick."

Ernie whispered something in Frederick's ear and then put the doll's mouth to his own ear. He grinned. "Frederick said nice to meet you, too."

Jane linked her arms with the other two men. "This is Paul and Gideon."

Paul's dark hair was combed away from his face. He had a smudge of paint on his left cheek. Paint stains splattered his royal-blue apron.

"Nice to meet you, Paul."

Paul nodded twice, gave Nick's hand two shakes and then took two steps back where he tapped on the wall twice. He dropped his gaze to the floor, but his lips moved as he talked to himself.

"Gideon, can you say hi to Nick?" Jane placed her hand on Gideon's back and urged him forward. He dug in his heels, crossed his arms over his chest and shook his head.

"You don't feel like talking?"

Gideon glared at Nick and shook his head again.

"Why not?" Jane spoke in gentle tones.

"He did the crossword puzzle." His bottom lip protruded.

Nick frowned. "What crossword puzzle?"

"My dad's puzzle."

The old man at Cuppa Josie's. A wave of heat crawled up Nick's neck. He cleared his throat. "I'm sorry, Gideon.

I didn't know your dad did the puzzle. I'm new in town. Please forgive me."

Gideon looked at Jane. "Do I have to?"

She shook her head and smiled. "No, it's your choice. I hope you do. I'm sure Mr. Nick would like to be friends."

"Okay, Mr. Nick, I'll be your friend." Gideon stuck out a chubby hand. Nick reached for it, but before he could shake it, Gideon wrapped his arms around Nick and hugged him. He laid his head on Nick's chest. "Thanks for being my friend."

Nick patted Gideon's back and prayed he didn't look as uncomfortable as he felt.

Jane cupped a hand around her mouth and spoke in an exaggerated whisper. "Gideon, I think you're surprising our guest. Would you like to help me work on a jigsaw puzzle while Mr. Nick talks with Mr. Walt?"

Once Jane had redirected the three men back to the living room, Walt turned to Nick. "You handled yourself well. Other than Gideon launching himself at you. That's important since I'm assuming you will be visiting quite a bit if you choose Jacob House for Ross's new home. The men are close. Their acceptance helps."

"I'll be here several times a week. My brother is an important part of my life."

Walt smiled. "I'm glad to hear it. Sounds good. Come on. Let's grab some coffee."

Walt led them through the living room. Ernie and Frederick sat on a dark brown leather couch, watching cartoons on the wide-screen TV. Jane and Gideon sat at a square table putting together a puzzle. Light streamed through a large bay window dressed in ruffled curtains, highlighting the pieces. Paul stood in front of an easel, holding a palette in his left hand as he added strokes of color on the canvas. A bird and a nest took shape.

Nick had seen similar paintings hanging on the wall at Cuppa Josie's. He watched Paul for a moment, then realized Walt waited for him near another doorway. He hurried across the room. "Sorry. He's quite talented."

"Very much so. Painting is part of his therapy. Paul has a form of autism. Come into the kitchen, and I'll get you some coffee. How about a slice of freshly baked cinnamon bread?"

"If it's as good as it smells, you won't have to ask twice." Nick followed Walt into the kitchen. An older woman wearing a pink apron helped a younger woman dressed identically turn out a loaf of steaming bread onto a cooling rack.

"Nick, this is my wife, Mae, who prepares all the meals, and our daughter, Tilly, who assists." Walt rounded the table and dropped a kiss on his daughter's cheek. "Mae, Tilly, this is Nick Brennan. He's the one Patty called about for his brother."

Mrs. Hoffman smiled as she flipped another loaf of bread onto a cooling rack. "Nice to meet you."

"Thanks, same here."

She turned to her daughter. "Tilly, can you say hi?"

Tilly shoved the chef hat out of her eyes and sidled closer to her dad. "Hi." She looked at him through her thick lenses and smiled.

She had the same physical features as Ernie and Gideon. Walt took a couple of brown stoneware mugs out of the cupboard next to the sink. "Pull out a chair. I'll tell you a little about Jacob House then give you the fifty-cent tour."

Grabbing the coffee pot, he filled both cups, setting one in front of Nick.

Stirring cream into his coffee, Nick went through his mental checklist of questions. He wished he could ask what really mattered—would they love Ross as much as he did?

Walt sat and extended his legs, crossing his feet at the ankles. "We provide constant opportunities for residents to be as independent as possible. Mae helps them cook and grocery shop. Jane and the other staff members help them with cleaning and volunteering in the community. We take them on daily outings to the library, the grocery store, the mall, the park. We want them to be able to participate in everyday life." Walt paused as his wife set a tray in front of them—thick slices of bread, a butter dish and a small jar of what appeared to be homemade jam. Walt nudged the tray toward Nick and continued. "Ernie works part-time at the bowling alley and Gideon helps out at Cuppa Josie's."

Cuppa Josie's? Interesting.

"How long has Jacob House been in operation?" Nick spread Mrs. Hoffman's whipped honey butter across his bread slice, trying not to linger on the fact Walt just dropped about Josie's.

"About eight years. It's named for our son, Jacob, who died at birth."

Nick froze as he was about to bite into his bread. He hadn't expected that. "I'm sorry."

"Thanks. Mae and I celebrated our fifteenth anniversary in Hawaii. Once back home, Mae came down with a bug, only to learn it wasn't a virus at all. She was pregnant with twins. Jacob and Tilly were born prematurely due to complications. Jacob didn't make it. Tilly spent a few months in the hospital. She was our miracle baby and has been a daily blessing from the day she was born."

Nick appreciated the look of love Walt wore as he spoke of his family. "You have a lovely family. How old is Tilly?"

"Twenty-two."

"A few years younger than Ross." His gut told him this was the right home for Ross—warm and loving. Exactly what his brother needed. But would Walt feel the same way when he learned how Nick destroyed his family?

The doorbell rang. A moment later, Josie appeared in the kitchen doorway, holding a box.

What was she doing here?

Would Walt notice if Nick slid under the table? Probably not the most mature move.

Mrs. Hoffman met Josie in the doorway and placed a hand on her shoulder to guide her into the other room, but not before Josie cast him a puzzled look. Probably wondering why he was drinking coffee with Walt.

Mrs. Hoffman returned to the kitchen with the box in her hands. "I'm sorry about that, Nick. I would have introduced you, but I didn't want to interrupt your talk with Walt."

"What's in the box, love?"

"She had extra doughnuts and brought them for the guys."

Walt turned back to Nick. "Josie's a sweetheart who owns a coffee shop in town. She has her hands full right now. Her daughter is ill. Poor little dear."

Nick didn't say that poor little dear was his daughter, too. In fact, he didn't say anything but concentrated on chewing the bread that seemed to have dried out his mouth. He needed to keep his two worlds separate for now.

Walt drained his cup. "Let's walk, and you can tell me about your brother."

Nick forced down the last of his bread and carried his cup to the sink. As he rinsed it, he said, "Like I said on the phone, Ross is twenty-six. Eight years ago he suffered a traumatic brain injury from a car accident that keeps him from living a normal life."

"Normal life is so subjective, wouldn't you say? Some of the men in the house have more normal lives than the rest of us. Your brother's disability altered his life, but that doesn't mean he can't have one."

For the next half hour, as they talked about Nick, Walt showed Nick the rest of the house—the two double bedrooms downstairs, the library, the game room and the full gym in the basement. He, Mae and Tilly used the second floor for their residence.

As they walked past Walt's office, he showed Nick his credentials—a master's degree in special education and state licenses for Jacob House. He opened a back door and gestured for Nick to step onto the back deck overlooking the yard. "This is our backyard. The men enjoy gardening, playing softball, grilling or just hanging out back here. We do monthly family events and encourage participation. You interested in getting involved? Patty mentioned you care for your brother on your own."

"Yes, he's all I've got." Or did until last night.

He leaned on the wooden deck railing and surveyed the snow-crowned natural border. A small utility shed sat in the corner of the yard.

He could picture a small garden plot. Or Paul with his easel painting birds splashing in the birdbath. Maybe Ross would like to help plant flowers or something.

"So how'd it happen?" Walt pressed his back against the railing and watched him.

Nick didn't pretend not to understand what the older man asked. He steepled his fingers and watched a cardinal land on bird feeder hanging from a low pine branch. "I came home from college to see Ross's championship basketball game. He scored the final point that won his team the victory. The team headed to the local pizza joint. I drove Mom and Ross."

A chill skated across his collar. The cold had nothing to do with the weather. "Ross was stoked because college coaches had seen him shoot that winning hoop. The light turned red. I hit the brakes, slid on a patch of black ice and lost control. We were T-boned by a half-ton pickup. Mom was killed instantly. Ross suffered a traumatic brain injury. And I walked away with bruised ribs."

Walt laid a hand on his shoulder and gave it a gentle squeeze. "I'm so sorry. You can't blame yourself. It was an accident."

A lifetime couldn't erase the memory of that night. Burying his mother while his brother fought for his own life was unforgivable. Every time he looked at his brother, he was reminded of his mistake. The mistake that cost his brother everything.

Chapter Five

Inviting Nick to dinner to meet her family had been a mistake.

And she still hadn't told Hannah the father she hadn't met was about to eat dinner with them tonight. *Way to go, Josie. Great mothering.*

A quick glance at the clock showed she had an hour to cook and talk to her daughter, leaving her with about fifteen minutes to freshen up. If only she had time to sneak in a soak in the tub.

After putting water on to boil, Josie grabbed one of the copper-bottom skillets hanging from hooks above the island and started frying sausage. She coated another pan with olive oil and sautéed onions and garlic. After adding minced fresh basil and thyme from her windowsill garden above the sink, she poured in a jar of homemade tomato sauce. Within minutes, the spices filled the room with their aroma. She added pasta to boiling water.

Her kitchen, a blend of old world and modern conveniences, soothed her—oatmeal-colored painted cabinets capped with green marble countertops and accented with warm reds and deep golds drew out the tones in the herb-patterned wallpaper border.

Hannah walked into the kitchen with her nose still in a book. No surprise there.

Steam billowed from the sink as Josie drained the cooked pasta. She returned it to the stove and glanced at Hannah. "Girl, how can you read and walk at the same time?"

Hannah shrugged. "It's a gift. I was at the best part and couldn't stop."

Josie combined the pasta, sausage and sauce in a baking dish, grated fresh Parmesan over the top and slid it in the oven.

"Would you put your book down and wash the lettuce and tomatoes, please." Josie eyed the purple-and-black-plaid newsboy cap perched at an angle on her daughter's head and tried not to focus on the shadows under her eyes. "Cute hat, by the way."

Marking her place, Hannah set the book on the island. "Thanks. Aunt Lindsey gave it to me today. But I still look like a freak."

If only Hannah could see beyond her insecurities to what Josie saw. "Would you please stop saying that? You are so far from looking like a freak. You just look a lot more like your baby pictures, that's all." Josie smiled to show she was teasing.

Hannah rolled her eyes and made an "I'm so not amused" face. "Funny."

Josie bowed. "I'm here every Thursday."

"Yeah. Yeah. And don't forget to tip your servers, right?" Hannah pulled vegetables out of the refrigerator, cradled them and closed the door with her foot.

"Hey, they have to make a living, too." Josie rinsed the colander she used to drain the pasta and set it next to the sink for Hannah.

"You're not making dumb jokes all through dinner, are

you?" Hannah washed the vegetables gently and placed them in the colander.

"I'm hurt." Josie filled the sink with sudsy water and washed the dirty pots and pans, laying them on a dish towel to dry.

"Whatev."

She wiped down the stovetop and counters, moving the round-bellied ceramic chef that held her cooking utensils. "Is the English language becoming so exhausting that people can't even finish complete words?"

"Mo-om."

She dried her hands and caressed her daughter's pale cheek with her thumb. "In all seriousness, sweetie, hair doesn't make a person beautiful."

"Yeah, I know. It's what's inside that counts."

"Do you remember what we read during yesterday's breakfast devotional?" She ignored the guilt that gnawed about skipping devotions this morning.

"Something about how we look at outer appearances, but God looks at the heart."

"Right, so you need to quit worrying about how you look and remember what's inside *does count*."

"I'm sure God wasn't bald, though." Hannah touched her hat. "What's for dinner?"

So like Hannah not to be a permanent guest at her own pity party.

"Baked ziti with sausage." Josie diced tomatoes and onions, then mixed in pressed garlic.

Hannah dried the separated Romaine leaves and tore them into small pieces into a salad bowl. "Are you making bruschetta?"

"Yep." She sniffed back tears from dicing the onion.

"What's for dessert?"

"Gelato in pizzelle cones." Josie minced basil before adding it to the rest of the vegetables.

"Wow, Mom, either you're in big trouble or tonight's really special. What's with making all of Grandpa's favorites?"

"You're being silly. I'm just making dinner."

"Pizzelle cones are saved for birthdays. And it's no one's birthday." Hannah crossed her arms and tapped her foot. "What did you do?"

"I didn't do anything. Why don't you set the table and stop bugging me?" Josie snapped her gently with the dish towel.

"You're sucking up."

"I am not." She was. But to whom? Her dad? Or Nick?

Hannah shrugged. "I'll find out sooner or later."

"Table." Josie pointed toward the dining room with her knife.

"Fine. I'm going. How many plates?"

Josie did a mental count in her head. "Nine. Grab a folding chair from the closet, too, would you?"

"Aye, aye." Hannah saluted and headed for the dining room. She paused, turned back to Josie with a scowl marring her sweet features. "Nine? Wait a minute. Who's all coming?"

"Grandpa, Grandma Grace, *Nonno*, Aunt Lindsey, Uncle Stephen, Tyler, You, Me." Josie ticked the names off with her fingers.

Hannah held up eight fingers. "That's eight. Who's the last one for?"

Nick.

Josie cringed and swallowed a sigh. She meant to talk to Hannah sooner, but started cooking and forgot. And now she had to spring it on her shortly before Nick was due to arrive. Really scoring points now.

Josie pushed away from the counter and pulled out one of the stools from the island. "Sit for a minute, sweetie, we have to talk."

"What's wrong?" Hannah's face paled to the color of cooked pasta. She dug at the purple nail polish on her thumb. "You're scaring me."

"I'm sorry." Josie cupped Hannah's chin. "Nothing's wrong. Not really. In fact, what I have to tell you could be an answer to our prayers."

Hannah climbed on the stool and hooked her feet under the rungs.

Josie grabbed Hannah's hands and squeezed. "Listen, kiddo, I've been open and honest with you from the day we learned about your leukemia, so I'm going to give it to you straight." She blinked away sudden pressure behind her eyes. She needed to stay strong for Hannah. "I'm not a match. Neither is Grandpa or *Nonno*."

Hannah's eyes widened. "You're still looking for your mother, right?"

"I am, sweetie, but I haven't seen her in over twenty years. I promise not to give up, though."

Hannah dropped her gaze to her fingers and continued to pick the remaining nail polish off her fingers. "So now what? Am I going to die?"

Josie cradled Hannah against her chest. "Oh, baby. Not anytime soon, if I can help it."

"So what do we do now? Wait for a match through the donor program?" The fear in Hannah's voice sliced through Josie's heart.

"There's one other option we can try." Josie blew out a breath. "This is harder than I thought."

Hannah pulled back, tilted her head and eyed Josie warily. "What is? Just tell me. I can take it."

Josie searched Hannah's eyes—eyes like Nick's. Could

she take it? Her daughter was a fighter. But this...well, only one way to find out. "I love you very much and will do whatever it takes to make you healthy again. We're going to beat this. When I learned I wasn't a match, I had to find your father."

Hannah stared at her, then whispered, "You found... my d-dad?"

Josie nodded, not trusting herself to speak.

"Where was he? How did you find him? What does he do? What's he like? Did you talk to him? Is he cute?" A sparkle twinkled in her daughter's brown eyes.

"Cute? Seriously? You remember a long time ago when you asked me about him?"

"Yes, you said he didn't want us."

"That's what I thought at the time. Turns out he didn't know about you. And talk about being surprised. We talked things out. His mother chose not to tell him that I wanted to get in touch about you."

"Why would she do that?" Hannah grabbed an orange from the ceramic bowl in the middle of the island and tossed it from hand to hand.

"Sweetie, sometimes grown-ups make poor choices. She must've felt she was doing the right thing by not telling Nick." Josie couldn't help but wonder what her motives were, but she'd never find out. If only she could take back her words from their conversation yesterday. In her defense, she didn't know he had lost his mother.

"When did you talk to him?"

"He came into Cuppa Josie's last night as I was closing." Josie removed the orange from Hannah's hands and returned it to the bowl.

"Then what happened?"

"I told him about you, the leukemia and the bone marrow transplant. He promised to get tested." No need to mention Nick's ludicrous marriage proposal.

"He did? Do you think…" Hannah's voice trailed off as she chipped away more polish.

Josie tilted up Hannah's chin. "Do I think what?"

"Do you think he'll like me??" Hannah's eyes filled with tears.

Josie gathered her in her arms. "Oh, baby, how could he not?"

"I'm not exactly pretty." A tear slid down her cheek.

Josie brushed it away with her thumb and choked back her own emotions. "Oh, honey, you are absolutely gorgeous."

"You have to say that because you're my mom." Hannah sniffed.

Josie cupped Hannah's chin. "I say that because it's the truth. And Nick thinks so, too."

Hannah wiped the back of her hand across her eyes. "He said that? How does he know?"

"I gave him a picture. Plus, he came to see you last night but you were asleep."

"I can't believe this." The corner of Hannah's lip lifted—another Nick trait. "I finally have a dad."

The smile that brightened her face almost made Josie feel guilty for not looking for Nick sooner. Almost.

"Sweetie, listen. I'm not going to push you to have anything to do with him unless you're ready. Take your time to get to know him."

"Are you kidding? This is, like, the coolest thing ever! I can't wait to tell Ashley."

"Are you sure you're okay with all of this? I'm so sorry to spring this on you at the last minute."

"Mom, it's cool." She gave Josie a quick peck on the cheek.

The doorbell rang. So much for freshening up. She didn't even have dinner completely ready. "Grab that, would you?" It's probably Grandpa and Grandma Grace."

Hannah slid off the stool and headed for the door. Josie returned to the counter and reached for the bread knife to slice the ciabatta bread when she heard Hannah say, "So you must be my dad."

Words escaped Nick as he stared into brown eyes that mirrored his own. She looked a lot different than she had last night curled in a ball, hugging a purple alligator. Or this morning at the coffee shop with her nose buried in a book. And she was his daughter. His breath escaped his chest as if kicked in the gut.

"Yes, apparently so." *Great line, man. Get in the game.* He tightened his grip on the wrapped bouquet of pink-and-white tulips he bought at the Forget-Me-Not floral shop across the street from Josie's coffee place.

Cocking her head, she gave him a once-over. "You were at Mom's shop this morning."

"Right." Another pithy line. "And you are Hannah."

"If not, I've been living here by mistake." Her lopsided smile created a dimple in her cheek. His breath caught in his chest.

Her mother's quirky sense of humor.

"You're just as pretty as your mom."

A pink blush added color to her cheeks. She ran a hand over her hat. "Thanks."

He shoved a hand in his coat pocket and nodded toward the house. "May I come in?"

"Yeah, sure. Sorry." Hannah stood back and held the door while he entered. "Are those flowers for my mom?"

"Yes, they are. I brought you something, too." Nick handed her a pink gift bag with a ballerina on the front. "I hope this is okay." He shifted his weight from one foot to the other. What does a guy buy for a kid he didn't know? Guess he needed to find out, considering he had years of gifts to make up for.

Scents coming from the kitchen forced his senses to wake up and pay attention. His stomach rumbled.

Hannah pulled a purple journal out of the bag.

"Thank you. I love it." Her dimple reappeared again as she smiled and ran a finger over the daisy in the corner of the cover. "Purple is my favorite color."

He'd guessed that from the purple in her room, the alligator she cradled and the purple "Princess in Training" long-sleeved T-shirt she wore. And the hat on her head.

He winked at her. Her smile warmed places in his heart he didn't know existed. Is this how it felt to be a dad?

"Nick. You're early."

Nick swung his gaze from his daughter to her mother standing in the doorway with a dish towel in her hands. Was that censure in Josie's voice?

He crossed the room and held out the flowers. "Here, these are for you." Did she still like tulips? During their first date, she had mentioned they were her favorite flower, so he sent her a bouquet a few days later. But that was over ten years ago.

"You didn't have to bring us anything." Josie buried her face in the blooms and inhaled. "They're lovely. Thank you."

The flowers weren't the only lovely things in the room. He'd have to be blind not to appreciate the way her jeans and white sweater flattered her figure. He fisted his hand in his pocket to avoid reaching up and undoing the clip that held her hair. He wanted to see it spilling over her shoulders again.

Don't go there, man.

"I hope it's not a problem. Me being early, I mean. I had more time than I expected. Can I do something to help?" Instead of standing here babbling like an idiot.

Josie shook her head, unleashing a stray curl. She tucked it behind her ear and gestured toward the couch. "Have a seat. Would you like something to drink? Iced tea? Coffee?" She turned and headed for the kitchen.

"Iced tea would be great, thanks."

He glanced at the taupe leather sofa, but his attention shifted to the gallery of black-framed photos lining the wall.

Hannah as an infant. Hannah as a toddler, wearing a ruffly pastel dress and holding a basket. Hannah missing her front teeth. Hannah dressed in a tutu and ballet shoes. A black-and-white portrait of Josie and Hannah.

And he'd missed every single moment.

His jaw tightened. Instead of dwelling on it, he headed for the kitchen where savory scents lingered in the air, teasing his palate. His stomach rumbled.

He had heard the kitchen was the heart of the home, and judging by the papers and magnets littering the front of the refrigerator and books piled at one end of the counter, Josie's kitchen was just that.

The kind of kitchen—make that home—he didn't have growing up. No boxed mac and cheese or TV dinners here.

His mother tried, but working two jobs left little time for home-cooked meals.

Josie reached for a clear vase from the cabinet next to the sink. Her sweater rode up, exposing a sliver of pale skin at her waist. Nick averted his eyes.

She filled a vase with water and arranged the tulips, pausing to finger one of the petals. Picking up the vase, she turned. Seeing Nick, she gasped and nearly dropped the flowers. "You startled me."

"I'm sorry." He took the vase and set it on the island. "I came in to talk to you for a minute."

"Okay, what's up?" She opened the fridge and pulled out a pitcher of iced tea.

"I had blood drawn today."

Josie's hand froze as she reached for a glass. She dropped her hand and gripped the edge of the counter, her head bowed.

He couldn't see her face. What was she thinking?

"Josie?" He touched her shoulder.

She shook her head.

Hadn't she wanted him to get tested? Women. Who could figure them out? Sighing, he plowed a hand through his hair and leaned against the counter. "I thought that's what you wanted."

She nodded and slowly turned to him, her eyes bright. A tear slid down her cheek, etching a trail to his heart. With a shaky hand, she brushed it away. "I'm sorry. I'm… Thank you. After last night…well, I wasn't sure what to expect."

"Look, I was an idiot, okay. I wasn't trying to give you an ultimatum or anything. Chalk it up to shock, I guess. I'm sorry. I can't make up the past, but I plan to be a part of Hannah's present and future. You don't need to handle this alone." He ached to draw her to his chest, knowing her head would tuck beneath his chin like perfectly fitted puzzle pieces.

But touching her was dangerous.

He shoved his hands in his pockets and inhaled the vanilla and freshly ground coffee fragrance that clung to her.

The doorbell rang. Josie gave him a nervous smile. She tucked loose strands of hair behind her ears and smoothed her sweater. "If you'll, uh, excuse me, I…uh…should see who that is."

She hurried out of the room, leaving Nick to follow. Shoving his hands in his front pockets, he leaned against the mantel, which allowed him full view of the front door. Josie hugged a tanned, silver-haired man and a beautiful woman with short blond hair. Josie's grandfather stood behind them.

The woman handed her coat to Josie and adjusted a sheer floral-printed scarf around the neck of her yellow sweater. "Smells great, Josie. You shouldn't have gone to all this trouble."

"No trouble at all. Besides, you and Dad are totally worth it. There's someone I want you to meet." Josie crossed the room and grabbed Nick by the elbow. "Dad, Grace, this is Nick. Nick, this is my father, Max Peretti, and my stepmom, Grace. You met *Nonno* last night."

Glad he changed into Dockers and a button-down shirt before leaving the hotel, Nick stepped forward and extended his hand to Josie's grandfather. "Nice to see you again, sir."

Josie's grandfather speared Nick with a narrow-eyed glare, but nodded and shook Nick's hand, anyway, before shuffling to the worn recliner in the corner of the room.

So much for his approval. Nick turned to the rest of the family. Josie's stepmom's quick smile and kind eyes put him at ease. A little. "Nice to meet you, Mrs. Peretti." He held out his hand to Josie's father. "Mr. Peretti."

Mr. Peretti gave his hand a firm shake. "Nick. Have we met? You seem familiar."

Nick cast a sharp glance toward Josie. She stepped forward. "Dad, um, you have met Nick before. You see—"

"Grandpa!" Hannah paused on the stair landing, then rushed down the last three steps before hurling herself at her grandfather. "I'm so glad you're home. I missed you so much."

Would Hannah ever react that way with him? Nick extinguished that spark of envy at their tight relationship.

Mr. Peretti engulfed her in a hug. "Hey, Banana. You get prettier every day. How are you feeling?"

"Pretty good. Especially now that you and Grandma Grace are back."

He flicked the brim of her hat. "We were gone just a couple of days."

"A couple of days feels like forever." She turned to face Nick. "Did you meet Nick?"

"Yep, just now." Mr. Peretti smiled at his granddaughter. "Isn't it so cool?"

"What is, sweetheart?"

"That Nick is my dad." Hannah shot him another one of those lopsided smiles he was growing to love.

Mr. Peretti jerked his head from Hannah to Nick to Josie. His eyes narrowed. "Your *what?*"

Even though he kept his tone even, Hannah's excitement evaporated as she glanced at each of the adults. "D-didn't Mom toll you?"

Josie touched Hannah's shoulders. "I was just about to, but you beat me to it."

"I'm sorry." Hannah chipped at her nail polish.

"Hey, you did nothing wrong. How about setting the table for me? Remember red square plates with the green-and-gold ones."

"Okay." Hannah left the room, but with much less enthusiasm than she showed on the stairs. Nick had an overwhelming urge to follow and wrap her in his arms. The look on her face pierced his heart. It wasn't her fault her parents screwed things up. Why did the kids have to suffer? He'd give up his last breath before he hurt her again.

Mr. Peretti stood with feet apart and wrapped an arm

around Josie's shoulders as if to show Nick exactly where she belonged. "So, what's going on here?"

Josie slipped out of her father's embrace and waved toward the couch where her stepmother sat. "Dad, sit down."

"I don't think I want to." He continued his drill instructor stance, glaring at Nick.

"Please."

"Come on, Max. Sit down and let Josie explain." Mrs. Peretti tugged on her husband's arm, her brows knitted with concern.

"Fine." He tugged on his pant legs before sitting and nodded to Nick. "You'd better have a good reason for suddenly showing up after all this time. What's the matter with you, anyway? You got my daughter pregnant and disappeared for ten years."

Nick took a step forward. "Sir—"

Josie pressed a hand against Nick's chest. "Wait." She knelt in front of her father and grabbed his hands. "The results came back. I'm not a match."

"Oh, Josie. I'm sorry, honey." He laid a hand aside her cheek.

She bit her lip and nodded. "After I learned my marrow didn't match Hannah's, finding Nick was my last hope. Agnes suggested checking out Facebook. I found out he was an English professor at Linwood Park University, so I went to see him. He came to the shop last night as I was closing up, and we talked." She paused, then cleared her throat. "He didn't know about Hannah."

Mr. Peretti's head snapped up. "How's that possible? You told his mother. She promised to contact him myself."

"I did, but she chose not to pass on the news."

Mr. Peretti eyed Nick. "Is this true?"

"Yes, sir."

Rubbing his forehead, Mr. Peretti leaned forward, resting his elbows on his knees. He stared at the carpet for a moment, then looked back at Nick. "Are you married? Dating anyone?"

Even though the scowl didn't leave Mr. Peretti's face, Nick sensed his attitude shifting. Just a bit. "No, sir."

"Have any other children?" His glare could melt ice.

"Not that I know of." As soon as the words left Nick's mouth, he wished he could snatch them back and cram them down his throat.

Josie's father jumped to his feet, his hands fisted as he took a step toward Nick. His contorted face matched his red V-neck sweater. "You find this funny, son?"

Mr. Peretti stood so close Nick could see the man's pupils contracting. He gulped. "Not at all, sir."

"Then why the smart-mouthed answer?" Mr. Peretti stepped closer to Nick.

A throbbing in the back of his head intensified, wrapping his brain in a headlock. Before he could open his big mouth and rectify the situation, Josie jumped between them, planting a palm on each of their chests. Her voice hissed. "Knock it off. Both of you. Dad, relax. Nick didn't mean anything by it. Hannah doesn't need the two of you going at it. She's been through enough already." Her eyes shot toward the dining room.

Nick's neck heated. His daughter was in the other room and he was ready to tangle with her grandfather? What a way to win the kid's approval.

Mr. Peretti's shoulders relaxed. He took a step back. His face softened as he looked at his daughter. He scrubbed a hand over his head. "What are your intentions now, Nick?"

"Dad..." Josie's voice held that "I'm warning you" tone.

Nick admired Josie's strength and her relationship with

her family. But he could fight his own battles. He was man enough to own up to his mistakes. Although this probably wasn't a great time to mention he had crashed and burned in the marriage proposal department. "That's up to Josie and Hannah. I'm willing to be as involved as they will let me. I have other business in Shelby Lake, so I'll be here often."

Mr. Peretti sat next to his wife and draped an arm over her shoulders. "Linwood Park is quite a ways, isn't it?"

"About ninety minutes, but I need to be in Shelby Lake every other day, anyway."

"Why?"

Tired of Mr. Peretti's inquisition, Nick wanted to tell him it was none of his business, but didn't think that would fly. Ross's face flashed through his thoughts. What would Josie's dad have to say about that? And Josie? If she knew the truth, would she even let him around Hannah? He couldn't risk it. Not yet. "Family obligations."

The doorbell rang again, giving Nick a breather. Honestly, he couldn't blame the guy. If some chump messed with his daughter, he'd be all over him. Trouble was Max wasn't going anywhere, and a lifetime of grief would be hard to swallow. Nick dropped into a leather armchair and rubbed a thumb and forefinger over his eyes.

Someone clapped a hand on his shoulder. He looked up to find Josie's grandfather standing over him. Was this round two?

"You seem like decent man. Don't let the past repeat itself."

"You have my word, sir." At least somebody in the room wasn't ready to lynch him.

"Break their hearts, you answer to me." The man's clipped accent emphasized his promise.

He needed to earn more than just Josie's trust again.

Even though he'd learned about Hannah less than twenty-four hours ago, he understood the protectiveness the two Peretti men felt for the women in their family. The thing was, though, how did he make them understand hurting Josie or Hannah was the last thing on his mind?

Chapter Six

"Burt, please, just one more week. I'll have all of the money by next Friday." Josie clutched the cordless phone as she stood on tiptoes to reach the bag of chocolate chips.

"I'm sorry, Josie, but you were late the past two months. I know you're going through a rough patch right now, but my hands are tied."

"Burt, really? My daughter has leukemia. That's a little more than a rough patch. By the way, how's *your* family?" She grabbed a long-handled wooden spoon and tried to push the morsels to the edge of the tall industrial metal cart.

With all of the construction going on in the storeroom, she'd had to move all of her supplies into the kitchen, making the small space even more crowded. The best storage option was to go up. She pulled out a plastic tote of flour and stood on the end, testing to see if it would hold her weight.

"I'm sorry, Josie. If your mortgage payment isn't here by the close of business tomorrow, your loan defaults."

Josie ended the call and shoved the phone in the pocket of her apron. She rested her forehead against the cold metal. When would she catch a break? When did life become so hard? All she wanted was a healthy daughter and thriving business. Was that too much to ask?

Throwing herself a pity party was not going to get the baking done. Without a full pastry case, she wouldn't generate an income. No income meant no business. No business meant no insurance. No insurance meant her daughter's life was even more at risk.

She and Hannah had a girls' night planned with Grace, Lindsey and Hannah's best friend, Ashley. Movies, pedicures and popcorn. But first, she had chocolate chip muffins and an apple crisp to make—no, make that two apple crisps since that was tomorrow's special.

One more inch and she'd be able to reach those chips—

"What are you doing?"

Nick's deep voice startled Josie. The spoon flew out of her hand and clattered to the floor. Her arms pinwheeled as her foot slipped off the end of the tote. Instead of landing on the floor, she fell against a hard chest. He smelled of soap and leather. Her stomach flip-flopped.

She pushed away from him, her heart thundering against her rib cage. "What are you doing?"

Nick released his hands from her forearms. "I think I asked you first."

"Hanging wallpaper. What does it look like I'm doing?" She turned away and eyed the blasted bag of chocolate chips hanging over the edge, mocking her.

"Trying to break your neck." Nick strode to the shelf, reached up and snagged the bag. He turned and dropped it on the counter.

Of course, he made it look so easy.

She strode to the calendar hanging by the door and ran a finger along the filled-in squares. "Neck breaking? Was that today? I thought I had that penciled in for tomorrow. You're right—that was on today's to-do list, wasn't it?"

He leaned against the counter, crossing his arms and ankles. "What's with the attitude?"

Josie sighed and sagged against the wall, not liking the way Nick appeared to fit in her kitchen. "I'm tired. And cranky. And feeling claustrophobic in my own kitchen."

She wasn't about to mention her phone call to Burt. That was her problem. She'd find a way to get the money.

"Maybe you need a better storage system." He eyed the racks and stacks of totes.

"There's no room." Having his six-foot frame in the room didn't help with space, either. Her supplies weren't the only things making her feel closed in. Seeing Nick almost every day didn't do her heart any favors.

"Make room. How can you work if your space isn't efficient?" Nick took off his coat and hung it next hers by the back door. He stood with his back to her, hands on his hips, and surveyed her racks and totes.

"With everything going on, I just don't have the time." She ripped open the bag of chocolate chips and scooped out enough for her muffin batter.

"Let me help. I can do it for you."

"No, thanks."

"Josie, you spend so much time taking care of others. When are you going to take care of yourself?" Nick stood behind her and placed his hands on her shoulders. He used his thumbs to massage circles in the base of her lower neck.

Please stop.

Don't stop. Ever.

Josie closed her eyes a moment, savoring the gentle strength in Nick's hands on her neck. All she had to do was lean back about an inch, and she'd be in his embrace. Three more seconds and she'd be as strong as her muffin batter, which wouldn't be good for either one of them. With a sigh, she stepped away from him. Reaching for the bowl, she folded in the chips, then scooped batter into the muffin tins. "When my daughter is healthy, and my business is in the black."

"I'm sorry." Nick pulled a scoop out of the large crock of utensils on the counter and helped fill the muffin tins.

Josie laid a hand on his arm. "I'm sorry for biting your head off. Not your fault."

"At least I understand why Agnes is caring for the front of the store." He smiled, his eyes crinkling at the corners. Her stomach flip-flopped again.

Josie opened the oven and slid the muffins onto the rack. Closing it, she set the timer. "Yeah, she banned me from the dining room. My own store. I think she forgets who's in charge sometimes."

"And you wouldn't have it any other way." Nick carried the empty bowl to the sink. He paused to push up his sweater sleeves before dipping his hands into the sudsy water to wash her latest batch of dishes.

"No." Why did he have to look so at-home doing her dishes? She forced her eyes away from the way his sweater stretched across his broad shoulders. "Why are you here, Nick?" She paused and held up a hand. "Wait, I didn't mean it that way. It's just you usually wait until evening."

Nick rinsed his hands, and then reached for a paper towel. He leaned against the sink and looked at Josie, his eyes becoming overly bright. "I just got a call from the doctor's office." He paused and swallowed. "I'm a match, Josie."

Match. He said match. A surge of warmth that had nothing to do with the heated kitchen rushed through her, filling those cracks where her heart had split open so many times over in the past year.

"Oh, Nick…" Her chest hitched. Tears filled her eyes. "This is an amazing answer to prayer."

Thank You, God.

Nick wrapped his arms around her. "Hey, come on. Don't cry. This is a good thing, remember?"

Nodding, she buried her face in the fibers of his sweater and slid her arms around his waist.

Their first glimmer of hope.

Her daughter had a chance. Correction—their daughter.

All because of Nick.

Nick tilted her chin and thumbed away a tear. "Are you okay?"

How did she thank someone for saving her daughter's life?

She stared at her feet a moment, then looked at him. "Thank you, Nick. I mean it. You have no idea how much this means to me. To Hannah."

"No thanks needed, Josie. I'm her father. I'm here for her. And you." He tightened his hold on her.

Josie chewed on the inside of her lip. But for how long? Life proved love didn't stick around. Her mother walked out when Josie was six. *Nonna* died when Josie was sixteen. And Nick. He'd left once. How long before he did it again? Was Hannah the only reason he was willing to stay put for now?

Josie shifted her gaze to the curve of his bottom lip. All she had to do was lift herself about two inches—

The timer dinged.

Jerking out of his embrace, she shoved her trembling hands in the oven mitts and pulled out the muffins. Heat crawled up her neck.

What was she doing, practically throwing herself at the guy? She probably looked like a worn-out circus clown with her smeared makeup and red nose.

If she closed her eyes, she could flick through her memories and pull out the day he broke her heart and relive that pain as a reminder to keep him at arm's length. Repairing her broken heart had taken more time than she cared to admit.

Nick touched her shoulder. Josie forced herself not to shrug his hand away. "How about if I pick up a pizza and a movie? We could celebrate at your house."

"Could we do it another night?" She flipped the muffins out onto cooling racks and lined them in rows. "Hannah's been looking forward to the girls' night we planned a few days ago." And *she* needed a break from his closeness.

"Sure, that's fine." By the look on his face, she guessed he assumed she was trying to give him the brush-off. Not really. Although her heart could use some distance from that mesmerizing smile.

She placed a hand on his arm. "I'm not making excuses. What about this weekend? We could make homemade pizza—my grandmother's recipe—and watch a movie. Hannah will love it."

He shrugged, acting as if it was no big deal, but she had seen the sparkle return to his eyes. "Okay, yeah. Sure, that'll be good. Anything in particular you want to watch?"

Josie shook her head. "I'll see if there's something new Hannah wants to see."

"I'm putting in a request at work for family leave. Like I've said, I want to be here for you and Hannah. You don't have to handle this alone anymore."

Despite the warning screaming in her head, Josie wrapped her arms around him again. Her head rested against his chest. His heartbeat thudded—*trust me, trust me, trust me.* Oh, how she wanted to cling to his promises.

She had to remember this was for Hannah. He wasn't interested in being her everyday Joe. After all, what they had ten years ago was over. They'd both changed, moved on with their lives. Despite being drawn to him, she couldn't afford to risk her heart again.

He made a promise to Josie and would do whatever it took to keep it—even put his job on the line.

Nick rapped two knuckles against the frosted pane of the open wooden door. "Dr. Clark, do you have a minute?"

Dr. Clark looked up from his desk, pulled off his wire-rimmed glasses and waved Nick into the room. "Dr. Brennan, you're giving me a good excuse to take a break. Have a seat, and tell me what's on your mind."

Nick entered the small room and settled in one of the studded leather chairs in front of the department head's desk. He tried not to squirm as the older man watched him. Was this how kids felt in the principal's office?

Leaning forward, he braced his elbows on his knees and fixed his eyes on the towering stack of binders teetering near the edge of the cluttered wooden desk. "Sir, I wanted to let you know I've submitted a request for family medical leave."

"Oh? Problems with your brother?" Dr. Clark stuck the stem of his glasses between his teeth.

"My brother's group home is closing, but I found another residence for Ross in Shelby Lake."

"Shelby Lake? That's quite a distance." Dr. Clark frowned.

"Yes, sir." Nick wiped his clammy palms on his Dockers.

"I can certainly understand your need to take care of your family. You'll have to file your request with human resources."

"Yes, I've already done that. I wanted to let you hear the news from me."

"I appreciate that, Dr. Brennan. I know what it's like to want the best for your family. It's too bad about your brother's home." Dr. Clark set his glasses on an open book, then leaned forward on his arms. "If I may be bold, you look like a man with more on his mind than your brother."

Nick scrubbed a hand across his face. "I've been given some news that has changed my life."

"Are you sick?"

"No, not me." Nick loosened his tie and unbuttoned the top button to his dress shirt. Was it warm in here? He sucked in a deep breath, grasping for a thread of courage to divulge the newly discovered skeleton from his past. He wasn't trying to hide his relationship with Josie, and now Hannah, but after hearing Dr. Clark rant for the past eight months about one of the other professors who caused a scandal by getting involved with a student, Nick wanted Dr. Clark to hear his news firsthand. Now if only his gut would stop rolling.

"Dr. Brennan?"

"I have a daughter." The words choked out of his throat as if someone had pounded on his back to dislodge an object blocking his breath.

Dr. Clark's eyes narrowed. His chair creaked beneath his weight as he sat back to digest the information. His lips thinned and nostrils flared, but he didn't say a word.

Nick could only imagine what the older man was thinking.

"Ten years ago when I was a senior in high school, I dated a girl for about a year. Our relationship ended before I started college. I didn't want her to feel tied down when I was a couple of states away. I thought I was doing the right thing. We spent one night together. She ended up pregnant, but I didn't know about the baby. She went to my mother, asking for my address, but she wouldn't give the information to Josie. Instead, she said she'd pass on the message to me, but she didn't."

"And now you learned about this daughter?" Dr. Clark raised an eyebrow and shifted again in his chair.

"A beautiful daughter who has leukemia. I've been tested, and I'm a match for a bone marrow transplant. Her doctor wants to start the transplant process soon." When Dr. Clark didn't say anything, Nick continued, "I've missed out on nine years of her life. I don't want her mother to go through this alone. They've been through so much already. My daughter is my responsibility."

Dr. Clark dragged himself to his feet and sauntered to the window. With his back to Nick, he shoved his hands in his pockets and jingled change in his pockets. "Your revelation puts this university in an awkward position."

"In what way, sir?"

"A small conservative college like ours depends on denomination support. If word gets out that one of our professors has an illegitimate child, I'm afraid that could have damaging consequences."

"But, sir—"

Dr. Clark cut him off. "We're already dealing with the backlash from Dr. Dole's escapade with that student. The daughter of one of our biggest supporters, might I add. I'm just not sure we could survive another scandal."

"Let me get this straight, sir. I've been with Linwood Park for the past four years with a stellar record. I tell you my daughter is dying of leukemia and needs a bone marrow transplant to survive and you're worried about the reputation of the university?"

Dr. Clark half turned to face Nick. His bulldog jowls sagged like stretched-out socks. "Now, Dr. Brennan, you're twisting my words."

"Perhaps you should straighten them out for me." Nick

took time to pull himself to his full height and forced a civil tone. "Are you saying my job is at risk, sir?"

"I'm sure, in time, you will understand the wisdom of what I'm saying."

The room with its dark paneling, tall bookcases stacked with dusty tomes and hard leather furniture closed in on him. He needed fresh air and sunlight—something, anything to restore the oppression in the room.

"Unfortunately my daughter doesn't have enough time to wait for your wisdom to sink in. What happened to grace?"

Chapter Seven

Standing with his back pressed against the counter in his small apartment kitchen, Nick swallowed a groan at the look of panic that skittered across his brother Ross's face.

"What about my friends? And my room? Where will I sleep?"

Nick opened the fridge and pulled out the milk. He checked the date before pouring a glass for Ross. He put a bendable straw in the glass and set it in front of his brother.

"Miss Patty needs to be with her family right now."

"But I love Miss Patty. She loves me. We're her family." With shaky hands, Ross pulled his digital camera out of his jeans and took a picture of his milk and cookies. Then he turned and took another one of Nick standing at the counter.

"You're right, she does love you. And Miss Patty does think of you as family, but her daughter needs her, too."

Dressed in jeans and a blue long-sleeved pullover shirt, Ross looked like any other guy his age. If only… With his short-term memory loss, slurred speech and uncoordinated muscle movements due to his traumatic brain injury, Ross wasn't like other guys his age.

"I don't want to go." Ross broke the chocolate chip

cookie Nick had bought at Cuppa Josie's into pieces. "I don't want to leave my friends."

"You'll make friends with the guys at Jacob House." Nick pulled out a kitchen chair and straddled it. "Walt likes to whittle. You like to whittle. Paul paints. Ernie likes to bowl. And Gideon likes to put puzzles together. You love puzzles."

"I like to do puzzles with Miss Patty." Ross's jaw tightened.

Nick stifled a sigh, forcing himself to remain patient with his brother. None of this was Ross's fault. The blame rested on Nick's shoulders. "You will be sharing a room with Gideon."

"What if they don't like me?"

"Why wouldn't they?" Nick placed a hand on Ross's shoulder. "You're a great guy."

"What if my friends forget me?" Ross picked up his camera and flipped through the pictures of the friends at his current adult care home.

"I'll help you stay in touch."

"You promise?"

"Of course. Anything for you." Whatever it took to make his brother happy. Ross was the only family he had.

Not anymore.

He had Hannah. Another reminder of how well he screwed up.

Ross put a broken piece of cookie in his mouth and chewed. "Will you wear a cape when you come to visit me? So my friends will know you're Super Nick?"

"But I'm not Super Nick, Ross." Nick stood and pushed in the chair. He shoved his hands in his pockets, wrapping his fingers around the Superman key chain Ross gave him one year for his birthday. If only his brother could realize failures weren't heroes.

"You are to me."

Ross's words washed over him as he stared out the small kitchen window over the sink. Gnarled oak limbs hunched like old men against the crisp March wind. Raindrops skated over the knobs and bends to the ends of the branches, hesitating a fraction of a second before dropping off the end in a free fall to the ground.

That was how he felt—as if he was free-falling.

Josie had less than two hours to prove she was a woman of her word. If she was late...no, she couldn't think about that right now. She *had* to make the mortgage payment on time this month.

But no matter how many times she added the figures, the number was still the same. And she was short by three hundred dollars.

Josie picked up a picture of Hannah taken at the lake. She traced a finger over Hannah's sunburned nose and sideways grin.

Nonno's favorite passage from Matthew whispered to her heart, *"Come to me, all you who are weary and burdened, and I will give you rest. Take my yoke upon you and learn from me, for I am gentle and humble in heart, and you will find rest for your souls. For my yoke is easy and my burden is light."*

When they learned about Hannah's leukemia, *Nonno* prayed that passage over them every night. Yet, Josie still treaded through her days, trying to keep her head above water. All she had to do was let go. And let God. She visualized treading water and letting go of a rope that she had been gripping with all of her strength.

Why was faith so easy to have when things were going well?

Replacing the frame on her desk, she leaned back in

her chair, covered her face with her hands and fought the scream rolling around in her throat. An ache pulsed in the pit of her stomach.

She had no other choice. The irresponsible daughter had to call her dad for a loan that she had no idea when she could pay back.

Dragging her fingers through her hair, she picked up her cell phone, scrolled to her dad's number and hit Send. And got his voice mail. Terrific. Now what?

She heaved herself out of her chair and walked into the kitchen. Not seeing Agnes, she headed to the empty dining room.

Agnes sang "It Is Well with My Soul" to herself as she sprayed the glass panel on the front door and wiped it clean. Without disturbing her friend, Josie shoved her hands in her front pockets and stared out the front window, listening to Agnes's words.

Yesterday's rain had frozen overnight, producing slick roads and a two-hour school delay. Giant snowflakes frosted the sidewalk like a sheet cake. Businesses would be letting out soon. The sidewalks would be full of people hurrying home. Maybe a few would stop in to grab a hot drink before braving the rest of the cold. Could she make three hundred dollars in the next hour? Not likely.

Agnes gathered the glass cleaner and paper towels. She turned and jumped, dropping the paper towels. She pressed her palm against her chest. "Gracious sakes, Sugar Pie. You nearly sliced ten years off my life."

"Sorry. I thought you heard me coming." Josie swallowed hard to choke back the lump in her throat.

"I was watching the snow and not paying attention." Agnes cocked her head and gave Josie a piercing look. "What's got you looking downer than a groundhog in February?"

Josie waved a hand over the empty dining room and sighed. "Ten customers. That's all we've had since lunch. I don't know, Agnes. Is it worth it anymore?"

Agnes nodded toward the street and wrapped an arm around Josie's shoulder. "Sugar Pie, take a look outside. Would you want to be out in that mess?"

"I've got to do something to generate some cash." In the stillness of the dining room, the steady ticking of the clock above the fireplace chipped away the remains of her hope. "Harv will have the apartment bathroom fixed and then I can rent it out again. Other than that, I'm not sure what else to do. But that won't help me today." She blinked away tears pricking the backs of her eyes. When did she become such a crybaby?

"Sugar Pie, if I had it to loan you, I'd do it in a heartbeat." Agnes laid a hand on her shoulder. "I do have a suggestion. Or two."

"Does it involve money?" Josie rested her cheek against Agnes's cool hand.

"Sort of."

"Giving it or receiving it?" She couldn't afford to spend a cent right now.

Agnes smiled. "Receiving it."

"Then I'm all ears."

Agnes pulled an envelope out of her apron pocket. "For starters, you should give this another gander."

Josie eyed the coffee rings on the envelope. Tightness squeezed her chest. "Ag, you know I don't do competitions."

"With those lacy-top drinks you serve, you'd be a natural at this." She took the envelope from Josie and removed a glossy brochure, advertising the Mid Atlantic Latte Art Competition. "Look here. It says a five-thousand-dollar grand prize. That kind of cash'll put a dent in your hairdo."

The baristas who smiled in the brochure as they swirled designs into their lattes made the art look so easy, but Josie knew from experience it wasn't the case. But five grand...wow, she could do a lot with that. "Any other time and I'd attempt it, but right now Hannah needs me. What else you got?"

Agnes shook her head, sending her fist-size hoops bobbing from her ears. She pointed toward the side staircase and the loft above the register that overlooked the dining room. "What do you think about renting the loft for morning Bible studies, afternoon book clubs or even crafting get-togethers? Maybe some of the locals would like to set up their art and handicrafts. You could sell their stuff on consignment or something."

As appealing as the idea was, the thought of adding one more thing to her schedule pressed weight on her shoulders. "That area is such a mess. Since the storeroom fiasco, I've been using the loft for storage. I don't know. Between baking, running the shop and caring for Hannah, when will I find time to take care of it?"

Agnes smiled, her eyes sparkling. "Don't you worry your pretty little head about it. I'll take care of cleaning it out and scheduling."

"Those are great options, Agnes, and I appreciate your willingness to help. But I need that extra money today. Plus, you spend enough time here. Don't you get sick of me?"

"Sick of you? Sugar Pie, you and that precious child of yours keep me from going batty at home. Besides, I refuse to let you do everything yourself. Letting those part-time high school girls go and cutting Gideon's hours while business slowed was understandable, but every minute you spend here takes you away from Hannah."

"I hate it, but right now, I have to work. If only God would give us that miracle I keep begging for."

"You keep praying. He'll keep answering."

The bells jangled against the glass as the front door opened. Nick walked in, stomping snow-covered feet on the mat and brushing snowflakes from his leather jacket.

He flashed that devastatingly handsome smile and nodded to them. "Hey, ladies."

"Well, aren't you a tall drink of water." Agnes purred as she gave him a once-over.

Josie swallowed, caught her breath and smiled back.

"Afternoon, Nick. Want some coffee?"

"Please. I stopped in to see if you needed a ride home. The roads are getting worse."

"Thanks, but my car drives great in the snow." She moved behind the counter and grabbed a mug, handing it to him.

"Okay, if you're sure." He took it from her, allowing his fingers to linger a second longer than necessary.

Josie pulled her hand away and grabbed the roll of paper towels Agnes had set on the counter. Tearing one off, she wiped down the spotless glass on the pastry case. "I am, but thanks again. You're welcome to drop by later, if you want. I'm sure Hannah would love to see you. Maybe we could play a game or something."

Josie, what are you doing?

Nick raised an eyebrow. "Is Hannah the only one who wants to see me?"

Over Nick's shoulder, Josie caught Agnes's exaggerated wink as she headed up the stairs to the loft.

Turning back to Nick, she smiled. "Well, *Nonno* has taken to you."

"Funny girl." He set the mug by the register and rounded the counter until he was two feet from her.

Josie swallowed and backed up, bumping into the espresso machine. She tucked a strand of hair behind her ear. "Funny-looking maybe."

An unreadable expression flitted across his features. She squirmed beneath his penetrating stare. He took another step closer and twirled a loose curl around his finger. "There's nothing funny-looking about you, June bug."

Her breath hitched at the mention of the nickname that caused images from high school to tumble through her mind. Bonfires. Homecoming games. Working late on the school newspaper. That fateful canoe trip where she overturned their canoe and earned the nickname of a pesky bug. But somehow he made it sound like an endearment. Simpler times.

"I can't believe you remembered." Was that breathless voice hers?

"How could I forget anything about you, Josie? You're the most incredible person I've ever met." He caressed her jaw.

"Maybe you need to raise your standards."

"Don't do that." His voice, still low and whispered, took on an edge. He cupped her elbows and pulled her to him. She placed a hand on his chest to keep some distance between them. "Do what?"

"Put yourself down. Just take my compliment and say thank-you."

"Thank you."

"That's better." Nick brushed her hair off her cheeks. "Your skin is so soft."

Words evaporated from her thoughts. She reached up and cupped his jaw, appreciating the scratchiness of his five-o'clock shadow. He smelled of early spring crispness, hope and promise of happily ever after.

Nick lowered his head.

"Josie—oh, pardon me."

Josie jerked, knocking her forehead against Nick's chin. She twisted out of his arms to find Agnes standing in the middle of the stairs, a grin the size of Texas splitting her face.

"Excuse me," Josie mumbled to no one in particular. She pushed through the kitchen door. She ran water into the sink, cupped her hands and splashed it over her flaming cheeks. She reached for a paper towel and buried her face in it.

The kitchen door swung open. Turning around, she found Agnes leaning against the counter, grinning at her.

"Don't look at me like that, Agnes Levine."

"Whatever do you mean, Sugar Pie? Can't a girl smile once in a while?"

"Right, like you're smiling just for the fun of it."

Instead of finding a solution to her financial situation, she allowed herself to get caught up in Nick's flirtatious charm.

"Oh, lighten up. It's about time someone put a spark in your campfire." Agnes pushed away from the counter and headed back to the dining room.

Yes, but her father taught her playing with fire was dangerous. And, of course, she didn't listen. And now she risked getting burned.

Chapter Eight

Nick knew how he could help Josie today, but he couldn't do it alone. He needed Agnes's help. But would she go behind her friend—and boss's—back to do it?

When Agnes returned to the dining room, Nick slid off the stool where he'd sat for the past seven minutes thinking about his almost-kiss with Josie. If only Agnes hadn't chosen that moment to come back downstairs. But he had to stop thinking about that. If he was going to help Josie, he needed to move fast.

Keeping an eye on the kitchen, Nick touched Agnes's elbow and lowered his voice. "Hey, Agnes, may I have a word?"

"Darlin', you keep smilin' at me like that, and I'll give you whatever you want." She placed a hand on her hip and trailed a polished nail across his chin.

He grinned, then cast a glance at the clock hands moving toward five o'clock. "I need a favor. I promise I have good intentions."

"What's up?"

"Who makes the daily bank deposits?"

Agnes tucked her flirt away and narrowed her eyes.

"Josie does. That poor darlin' gets frazzled about deposits. She says if something happens, it's no fault but her own."

"Could you get a deposit slip for me?" His eyes shifted to the clock. He had twenty-five minutes to pull this off.

"What's going on in that handsome head of yours?"

He glanced at the kitchen door to make sure Josie wasn't coming out and lowered his voice. "I came in through the back door originally and overheard the two of you talking about her mortgage being late this month. I want to help. I wasn't around when Josie really needed me so I want to make up for that. I'm sure she told you what happened between us."

"Sugar Pie, we've been talking about you from the moment you graced this place with those chocolate eyes and a smile that could light up a city."

"I want to pay her mortgage for a couple of months. I don't have her bank information. I doubt I can waltz in there and hand the teller a bag of money to put in Josie's account."

"Josie does her own deposits, but the tellers know me. I could make a deposit for you. How much of our conversation did you hear?"

"Enough to know she needs to make a payment by five, or it will be considered late."

"Well, then, we have no time to waste. Whip out that big ole white knight checkbook of yours." Agnes held out a hand, her rings glinting in the overhead lights.

"Thanks, Agnes. I appreciate this."

"Handsome, you're the miracle Josie's been praying for. She just doesn't know it yet. You're a hero."

Hardly.

He didn't deserve her praise. "This is nothing compared to what I should've been doing all of these years."

"Oh, posh, wasn't your fault your mama didn't do right

by you. What's important is you're here now. And you're helping. Just don't break their hearts."

"Agnes, I promise you—the last thing I want to do is hurt either one of them."

Less than a minute later, Josie pushed through the kitchen door. Spying him, she stopped. "Nick, you're still here."

"Your powers of observation could land you a prime spot on the police force."

"Hilarious. Don't give up your day job."

Nick grimaced. He had forgotten about his job. Dr. Clark's caustic words echoed inside his head. After the years of dedication he gave them, when he needed their support, he received threats about his job instead. Losing his job wasn't an option. He had Ross to care for. And now Hannah. Finding another position would be tougher due to budget cutbacks.

However, if he did lose his job, he wouldn't have to make a long commute almost daily to see Hannah or Ross. Or Josie. If he was honest, he'd admit he wanted to see her just as much. Now if only he could convince her to give him a second chance.

Three hundred lousy dollars was going to stand in the way of everything she needed right now. Hopefully she could reason with Burt.

With her heart sinking closer to her toes with every step, Josie pulled open the heavy glass door to the Shelby Lake Federal Bank. She crossed the patterned carpet, past the red velvet-roped waiting lines, and up three steps to Burt Sutter's office.

A quick glance at her watch showed she had ten minutes before the bank closed for the day. She knocked on Burt's open door.

Burt looked away from his computer and smiled. He stood, buttoned the top button to his suit jacket, covering his middle-aged paunch, and gestured toward one of the maroon upholstered chairs. "Good afternoon, Josie. Have a seat. What can I do for you?"

She perched on the edge of the seat and tried not to be distracted by the shine glistening off his dome ringed with a ruffle of dark hair. Looking over his shoulder, she focused on the Little League trophies lining the credenza behind Burt's desk. She took a deep breath and massaged the ache in her stomach. "I need to talk about my mortgage, Burt."

"Sure, how can I help?" He picked up a small bowl of wrapped peppermint hard candies and offered them to her. "Want one?"

Josie took a piece of candy—not because she wanted one, but because it gave her something to do with her hands.

"I know you said I couldn't have an extension." She unzipped the bank bag in her hand and withdrew wrapped bundles of cash. "Here's a partial payment. I'll have the rest by next week. I can't afford to lose my business, Burt. Not now. Not with Hannah..."

Burt moved out of his chair and circled around his desk. He rested a hand on her shoulder. "Josie, you must be working too hard or something."

She fought to keep from shrugging his hand away.

"What do you mean?"

"Your mortgage payment has been paid." He gave her one of those "bless your heart" smiles that Agnes saved for her duh moments.

"No, it hasn't." What was he talking about? She untwisted the plastic wrapping on the candy.

"Yes, it has. I looked at your account just a few minutes ago." Burt returned to his computer and clicked a few keys.

"There must be some mistake, Burt, because I haven't been in yet today." She popped the candy in her mouth, and was instantly reminded of Christmas.

He shrugged, keeping his eyes fixed on the screen. "Well, someone has because your account is definitely up to date and paid for April and May, as well."

"That's impossible. Are you sure you're not looking at someone else's account?" She fiddled with the zipper on her bank bag, trying to keep her fingers from trembling. It had to be a bank error. Or someone had access to her accounts.

Burt clicked another button on his keyboard. Within seconds, the printer spit out a sheet of paper. He grabbed it and handed it to her.

Josie looked over the paper and nearly choked on the candy. Definitely her account. Where did the five grand come from? Her money tree withered about the same time Hannah was diagnosed with leukemia. "Are you sure one of the tellers didn't deposit someone else's money in my account by mistake?"

"Excuse me a minute. I'll see if I can find the deposit slip." Whistling, Burt left his office, leaving behind a faint cloud of Aqua Velva.

Josie gnawed on her bottom lip and stared at the numbers on the paper. This didn't make any sense.

Burt returned a few minutes later, holding a deposit slip in his hand. "Josie, Cindy said Agnes stopped by about fifteen minutes ago with a large deposit for your account. She used one of your slips, so Cindy assumed you had sent her to make the deposit."

Chapter Nine

The second Josie's heart had softened against Nick, he pulled a stunt that proved he couldn't be trusted.

Hearing the doorbell, Josie gripped the countertop until her knuckles whitened. An hour wasn't enough time to get over his deception.

Hannah was excited to hear Nick was coming over. Josie had been looking forward to seeing him, too. But that was before she found about his sneaky, underhanded meddling into her business.

"Mom, Nick's here."

Josie turned to see Hannah pulling Nick into the kitchen by the hand. Nick balanced two pizza boxes. She leaned against the counter and crossed her arms over her chest.

"Where would you like these pizzas?" He smiled. But she wouldn't be sucked in by that grin.

"You pick, Nick. You're great at deciding what's best." Nick's brows furrowed. "What's that supposed to mean?"

Josie's gaze swung to meet her daughter's. "Sweetie, run upstairs and tell *Nonno* it's almost dinnertime and then go wash your hands, please."

As soon as she was sure Hannah was out of earshot,

Josie planted her hands on her hips and glared at Nick. "How dare you stick your nose in where it doesn't belong!"

"You're mad." Nick set the pizzas on the island and then leaned a shoulder against the refrigerator.

"How very astute, Professor." Josie nudged him out of the way to open the refrigerator. She pulled out the salad she threw together after she came home. Tearing lettuce did little to soothe her spirit, even when she pretended those leaves were Nick's neck.

"And sarcastic."

She slammed the salad bowl on the island. "What gave you the right to inquire about my financial information? That's private information. And none of your business."

She hated the relief she'd felt after prying the truth from Agnes. It wasn't a bank error. But Nick knowing about her financial situation bugged her more than she wanted to admit.

"I was just trying to help."

"I didn't ask for your help." Opening the dishwasher, she searched for the salad tongs. Not finding them, she closed it and hunted through the drawers, opening and closing without even seeing what lay inside.

Nick pried her fingers off the drawer pull and laced them with his. "That's the thing—you don't ask for anyone's help."

Josie jerked her hand away. "This was none of your business."

His jaw tightened. Over his shoulder, he pointed a thumb toward the kitchen doorway. "That child who just left this room? She *is* my business."

"Are you saying I can't take care of my own daughter?"

"*Our* daughter, Josie. You need to remember I'm a part of her life now."

"You didn't know she existed until I told you."

Nick gripped Josie's shoulders and gave her a gentle shake. "How many times are you going to throw that in my face? She's still my responsibility. And if you lose your business, her medical insurance is in jeopardy. That puts her health at risk. And are you willing for that to happen because of your stubborn pride?"

"This has nothing to do with pride." She pushed away from him and stared out the kitchen window. "You had no right to stick your nose in where it didn't belong."

"Would you listen to yourself? This has everything to do with pride, Josie. You're so bent on doing everything for yourself that your nose is out of joint because I stepped in to help. What's the big deal?"

She gritted her teeth and glared at him. "I didn't ask for your help."

"No, because you think you have to carry every burden by yourself." Gentling his voice, Nick rubbed a thumb and forefinger across his eyes. "You're not a pack mule, Josie. When are you going to look around and see how much people care about you? They want to help, but you're too stubborn to let them. You know, it's a sort of selfishness when someone isn't willing to let others have the joy of returning the gift of help and love."

"Oh, so now I'm selfish. I'm responsible for my own business. And you're a great one to talk about pride. You just want to gallop in on your white horse and save the day." Why couldn't he understand she couldn't count on anyone but herself? Otherwise, she'd end up disappointed. She couldn't really trust anyone. Not when it counted.

Josie pulled four glasses out of the cupboard and set them on the counter.

"You're right, but I'm jointly responsible for Hannah." Nick grabbed the glasses and pressed them under the ice dispenser. "I'm not walking away once this donor business is finished. Like it or not, you will have to deal with me for the rest of her life. Consider the bump in your account back payment on child support."

"I've provided for Hannah for the past nine years." She filled three glasses with tea, then grabbed the dishcloth to wipe up the condensation off the counter from the pitcher of tea.

"Woman, are you crazy? No one is questioning your parenting skills. You've done a terrific job." Nick swept an arm over the kitchen. "Look at this house—it's beautiful, welcoming and a real home, thanks to you. Hannah is well mannered, cared for and loved, thanks to you. I had nothing to do with any of that. But don't you see—I'm here to help. You just have to let me."

"You don't understand." How could she tell him she couldn't lose Hannah? If she loosened her grip, then things would spiral out of control.

"What's to understand? When was the last time you had a full eight hours of sleep? When was the last time you shopped for yourself, or had a girl's day out where your mind didn't focus on Hannah or the coffeehouse?"

Her energy drained from her body, leaving her feeling as limp as the wet dishrag in her hand. "Okay, so maybe you're right." She hated admitting that. "But you have no idea how I felt when I walked into the bank with a partial payment, ready to face Burt, only to learn my mortgage had been paid for the next three months."

Nick closed the gap between them and put his hands on her shoulders. "Josie, be honest. When you learned your mortgage had been paid for the next three months, what was your gut reaction?"

"There must've been some mistake. It was too good to be true." She refused to let his scent beckon her to come closer.

"And when you learned it wasn't?"

"Confusion about where the money could've come from—with a little relief. For once in my life, I had a cushion. I didn't have to worry."

"Good. Go with that feeling for now. You have enough to be concerned about without stressing about your mortgage. Come on, you know I'm right." A thread of pleading in Nick's voice nearly unraveled Josie's reserve.

Her shoulders sagged as she gave in and pressed her forehead against his warm chest, gripping the edges of his leather jacket. "Why didn't you just come to me? Instead of involving Agnes and going behind my back?"

His arms circled her, kneading the muscles at the base of her neck. "Then we would've had this argument at the coffee shop, and you would've missed your deadline. I twisted Agnes's arm to help me."

Josie scoffed, but smiled. "I don't think you had to twist very hard."

Nick tilted Josie's chin to meet her eyes. "She loves you and just wants to see things go a little easier for you."

"I just don't want to be indebted to anyone." She pulled her gaze away from those eyes and removed plates from the cabinet by the sink.

"Look, I'm sorry I went behind your back. I wanted to help. This is not a loan. Don't even think about paying it back. Consider it back pay for child support or something. I need to do more to help out. Maybe we should get papers drawn up or something. A man doesn't walk out on family."

"Is that what this is really about, Nick?" She'd been so stupid. "Trying to buy your daughter? Don't even think about trying to take her from me." Her fingers gripped the plates. "I will fight you with everything I have. I'm the one who raised her, clothed her, fed her, rocked her, comforted her—"

"Josie, get a grip, would you? Relax. I'm not taking her from you. She belongs here. You're a great mother. I'm not trying to disrupt her system, but I will help out financially, whether you like it or not."

He'd already proved he could go behind her back. Josie sighed and rubbed a hand over her forehead. "Fine. Then start a college fund. But don't buy her affection with expensive gifts. I can't compete with that. We've lived within a budget for years, and I like to think she's appreciative of what she has."

"Of course. And you have to promise to stop being so bullheaded and ask for help. Also, let me know if she needs medication or something that her insurance doesn't cover."

"Are you two done arguing yet? *Nonno* and I are hungry," Hannah said from the kitchen doorway.

Josie spun around to see *Nonno* standing behind Hannah with his hands on her shoulders. Hannah shifted from foot to foot. Her floral floppy hat shadowed her face, but Josie recognized the pouty lip her daughter had been perfecting since she was a toddler.

Josie's heart spiraled to the floor. So much for that Mother of the Year award. "We weren't arguing."

Hannah closed her hands into fists and stamped her foot. "I wasn't born yesterday, you know." Hannah's eyes filled with tears. "You're fighting because of me. I hate being sick. I'm ruining everything." She turned and rushed away from the kitchen.

Josie shoved the plates at Nick. "I need to go after her."

Nick set them on the counter next to the pizza boxes. "Let me have a shot."

Josie looked at him. "But…" She was the mom. The one who kissed away tears, bandaged boo-boos and made her daughter's world right again. Except she hadn't been doing that great of a job lately.

"Please."

Nonno shuffled into the kitchen and touched Josie's elbow. "*Cara*, he is good man. Let him be part of her life. Let him see parenting is more than presents and pizza."

Mr. Peretti's approval gave Nick the hefty dose of courage he needed as he took the carpeted stairs two at a time. At least someone in Josie's family was in his corner.

Nick hesitated a second at Hannah's partially closed door. What was he doing? He didn't know how to parent. What would he say to his daughter? Josie should be in his place.

Blowing out a breath, he knocked on Hannah's door before pushing it open. He took in the white walls and pale purple curtains that contrasted with the plush deep purple carpet, white furniture and enough stuffed animals to outfit a pretend zoo. The nebulizer on her nightstand and the misting humidifier reminded him this wasn't a typical girl's bedroom. And his daughter was anything but typical. But he was more than fine with that.

Hannah lay sprawled across her purple comforter printed with white daises.

"Can I come in?"

She turned onto her side, dislodging her hat, and shrugged. "I guess."

The milky paleness of her face highlighted the bruises under her eyes. Nick's gut burned as he walked to the bed and sat on the edge. "I'm sorry you heard that. Your mom is mad because I did something behind her back."

"Yeah, I heard." Hannah pointed to the vent in the floor. "My room is over the kitchen. Not the best place for a private conversation. Store it away for future knowledge."

His kid had smarts.

Nick pushed himself off the bed and sauntered over

to a matching white bookcase. He stooped in front of the books and read the titles on the spines. "You like to read."

"Yeah."

He pulled a Nancy Drew book off the shelf and leafed through it, remembering the Hardy Boys books he borrowed from the library when he was about her age. The scent of paper soothed the ragged edges around his nerves. "What's your favorite?"

Hannah scooted off the bed and reached over his shoulder to grab a tattered book with a bunny on the cover. She handed it to him. *"The Velveteen Rabbit."*

He took the book and traced the bunny's ears on the cover. "Why's that?"

"Because the boy loved the rabbit even when he was dirty and had no more hair." Hannah sat in the wicker rocker near the window and picked at her nail polish. "The rabbit wanted to be real. When the rabbit asked if it hurt, the Skin Horse told him when you are real, you don't mind being hurt."

Hannah's simple explanation caused a lump to form in his throat. She was too young to understand life like this.

"Dad?"

Nick's head snapped up. Did he hear correctly? His eyes drank in the vulnerability in his daughter's dark eyes. "Yes?"

She gnawed on her lower lip, the way her mother did, and stared out the window "Since you said you're going to stick around, do you mind, I mean, can I call you that?"

Nick tossed the book on her pillow and crossed to the window. He dropped to his haunches in front of Hannah and reached for her hands. "Sweetheart, you can call me whatever feels comfortable to you."

"I like Dad."

"I like it, too." Nick's voice cracked. He dropped his

gaze to her tiny hands half-hidden in his large paws and brushed a thumb over her narrow fingers. He blinked back suspicious wetness. He had to be the luckiest guy in the world.

"Can I ask you something else?"

"Anything."

"Are you here only because I'm sick?"

Nick shifted to sit on the floor in front of the rocker.

"What do you mean by that?"

"Mom told me she contacted you because I need a bone marrow transplant. If you weren't a match, would you have gone back to your life?"

He wanted to pull her into his arms and shelter her from the harsh realities of life. But he'd be willing to bet his daughter knew more about life's realities than half the kids in her school. "Well, kiddo, I'll be honest and say learning about you was a shock. But I promise, I'm here because I want to be. I wish I had been here from the beginning. Things would've been different." He tapped the tip of her upturned nose.

"You *want* to be with me?" She glanced at him shyly, then ducked her head as if afraid to see the answer on his face. "Even when I look like a freak?" A blush colored her cheeks as she touched her head.

Nick tugged Hannah's hat off her head and tossed it on the bed.

She jerked, staring at him a moment with wide eyes before covering her head with her arms. "Why did you do that?" The hurt in her voice made his chest ache.

Grasping her hands again, Nick pulled her to a standing position. He sat on the bed and pulled her onto the bed beside him. He rubbed his hand over her downy-covered head, and tilted her chin up to meet his eyes. "Hannah Peretti, you are the most beautiful child I've ever had the privilege of seeing. You take my breath away." He blinked several times and swallowed again. "I look at you and thank God for the perfect gift He has given me."

Hannah's eyes filled with tears. "You think I'm beautiful?"

"You're gorgeous. You must get that from your mother. But you know what? Being beautiful doesn't come from the clothes you wear, the color of your eyes or how much hair you have. Being beautiful comes from within." Still holding on to Hannah, he leaned across the bed and snatched *The Velveteen Rabbit* off her pillow. "In this story, the little boy loved the rabbit even though others thought it was ugly. He was faded, ratty and dirty, but to the boy, the rabbit was real. Hannah, my love, you are beautiful from the inside out. I'm sorry not having hair bothers you, but I promise you are incredibly beautiful even without it."

A tear rolled down Hannah's cheek. Nick thumbed it away. She burrowed her face in his chest, wrapped her arms around his neck and cried against his shirt. He cradled her and squeezed his eyes closed to hold back the tears pressing against his eyelids.

Opening his eyes, he found Josie standing in the doorway with tears running down her face.

"Thank you," she mouthed.

He nodded and sniffed, tightening his arms around his daughter. She would never doubt his love again.

Chapter Ten

Sunlight streamed through the window, reflecting off the votives and throwing a fan of color across the counter.

Rays warmed Josie's back as she pinned this week's cards to the word wall. Two days behind, and she would've left last week's words up there if a customer hadn't asked about the new ones. At least someone read them.

The Tea Grannies—five older ladies, including her step-grandmother and Agnes's mama, from her church who took matchmaking seriously—sipped their tea and prayed quietly at their usual corner table. Soon they could hold their daily Bible study upstairs in the loft.

When Walt Hoffman from Jacob House heard about Agnes's plans to renovate the loft, he offered that he and the men come and lend a hand in exchange for lunch.

An offer Josie couldn't refuse.

The door opened, bringing in a crisp nearly spring-scented breeze. Josie inhaled and waved to Billy Lynn, Shelby Lake's fire chief and her dad's good friend. "Hey, Billy."

"Afternoon, Josie girl." He removed his baseball hat advertising the fire station and tucked it under his arm as he unzipped his jacket. "Saw some crocus shoots on

FREE Merchandise is 'in the Cards' for you!

Dear Reader,

We're giving away FREE MERCHANDISE!

Seriously, we'd like to reward you for reading this novel by giving you **FREE MERCHANDISE** worth over $20. And no purchase is necessary!

You see the Jack of Hearts sticker above? Paste that sticker in the box on the Free Merchandise Voucher inside. Return the Voucher promptly...and we'll send you valuable Free Merchandise!

Thanks again for reading one of our novels—and enjoy your Free Merchandise with our compliments!

Pam Powers

Pam Powers

P.S. Look inside to see what Free Merchandise is **"in the cards"** for you!

W e'd like to send you two free books to introduce you to the Love Inspired® series. These books are worth over $10, but they are yours to keep absolutely FREE! We'll even send you 2 wonderful surprise gifts. You can't lose!

REMEMBER: Your Free Merchandise, consisting of 2 **Free Books** and 2 **Free Gifts**, is worth over $20.00! No purchase is necessary, so please send for your Free Merchandise today.

Plus TWO FREE GIFTS!

We'll also send you two wonderful FREE GIFTS (worth about $10), in addition to your 2 Free Love Inspired® books!

FREE MERCHANDISE VOUCHER

**2 FREE
BOOKS
and
2 FREE
GIFTS**

Please send my Free Merchandise, consisting of
2 Free Books and 2 Free Mystery Gifts.
I understand that I am under no obligation to buy
anything, as explained on the back of this card.

☐ I prefer the regular-print edition
105/305 IDL FS4T

☐ I prefer the larger-print edition
122/322 IDL FS4T

Please Print

FIRST NAME

LAST NAME

ADDRESS

APT. #   CITY

STATE/PROV.   ZIP/POSTAL CODE

NO PURCHASE NECESSARY!

related content rotated 180°:

᠁ ᠁ (barcode)

THE READER SERVICE
PO BOX 1867
BUFFALO NY 14240-9952

POSTAGE WILL BE PAID BY ADDRESSEE

BUSINESS REPLY MAIL
FIRST-CLASS MAIL   PERMIT NO. 717   BUFFALO, NY

NO POSTAGE
NECESSARY
IF MAILED
IN THE
UNITED STATES

The Reader Service — Here's how it works:

Accepting your 2 free books and 2 free mystery gifts (gifts valued at approximately $10.00) places you under no obligation to buy anything. You may keep the books and gifts and return the shipping statement marked "cancel." If you do not cancel, about a month later we'll send you 6 additional books and bill you just $4.49 each for the regular-print edition or $4.99 each for the larger-print edition in the U.S. or $4.99 each for the regular-print edition or $5.49 each for the larger-print edition in Canada. That's a savings of at least 22% off the cover price. It's quite a bargain! Shipping and handling is just 50¢ per book in the U.S. and 75¢ per book in Canada.* You may cancel at any time, but if you choose to continue, every month we'll send you 6 more books, which you may either purchase at the discount price or return to us and cancel your subscription.

*Terms and prices subject to change without notice. Prices do not include applicable taxes. Sales tax applicable in N.Y. Canadian residents will be charged applicable taxes. Offer not valid in Quebec. All orders subject to credit approval. Books received may not be as shown. Credit or debit balances in a customer's account(s) may be offset by any other outstanding balance owed by or to the customer. Please allow 4 to 6 weeks for delivery. Offer available while quantities last.

▲ If offer card is missing write to: The Reader Service, P.O. Box 1867, Buffalo, NY 14240-1867 or visit www.ReaderService.com ▲

my way to the station this morning. Nature's postcard, announcing new beginnings. Spring won't be long now."

He ambled to the counter where Agnes rang up his order and handed him a mug. After filling it, he settled in one of the armchairs and snagged the newspaper off the side table.

She turned back to the word wall and pulled a card out of the envelope.

Trust.

She tapped it against her palm. New beginnings, Billy had said. Was God giving her a new beginning with Nick? An opportunity to have a complete family—one where she didn't have to carry her burdens alone?

After hearing Nick talk to Hannah the other night, she didn't doubt his love for their daughter. His gentleness calmed her anxiety. But how did he feel about her? She wasn't even quite sure how she felt about him.

"Josie girl, what's a five-letter word for *to have faith in?*" Billy glanced up from the newspaper and pointed his pen at her like a dagger.

Josie's eyes rolled toward the ceiling. *Really, God? Trying to tell me something here?*

"Trust?"

His lips moved as he counted the spaces. "That's it. Thanks."

Agnes's head bobbed as she wiped down the front of the coffee bar. She hummed "Trust and Obey."

Okay, God. I get it.

As Josie stepped off the chair, the front door opened again.

Nick walked in, one hand still clutching the doorknob, and searched the room. His eyes connected with hers. He closed the door, nodded to the Tea Grannies and strode over to her. His bomber jacket hung open to reveal a brown-and-white-striped shirt left unbuttoned over a brown T-shirt. With his thumbs hooked around the front belt loops of his loose faded jeans, he appeared casual to anyone walking behind him. "Hannah said something's wrong with your tire."

"Hello to you, too. I'm fine, thanks. How's your day going?"

"Josie." His eyebrows puckered his forehead.

"I had a flat before I left the house and replaced it with a spare." Josie tucked the word envelope in her apron pocket and returned the chair to the table.

"That doughnut tire isn't meant to be driven on for any length of time. You need to get it fixed." He followed her as she made her way to the counter.

She shoved the envelope in the drawer under the register. "I will as soon as I can. It's fine for now."

Nick followed her to the counter. "Where's the flat tire?"

"In my trunk."

"Give me your keys and I'll get it fixed now." He held out his hand.

"I'm on my way to get her now. That tire is nothing to mess with."

"I told you I will do it when I have time." She grabbed a sticky notepad and a pen. Glancing at the pastry case, she noted what needed to be baked for tomorrow. "Aren't you supposed to be with Hannah?"

"Relax, okay?" She waved a hand across the dining room. "I'm working, then heading home."

Nick crossed his arms and leaned against the register, looking entirely too comfortable. "You can't drive that car until you get a decent tire on it."

"I live five blocks away. It will be fine."

"What about Hannah? Have you thought of her?"

His thundercloud scowl hunched his brows over his narrowed eyes.

The apparent disapproval tugging down the corners of his mouth caused her stomach to clench. "Only every minute of her life. What's this really about, Nick?"

"Then don't be so irresponsible." He pushed away from the counter and stared down at her. "I don't want you taking chances with Hannah in your car. Until you get that tire fixed, I'll take her or the both of you wherever you need to go."

The air whooshed out of Josie's lungs. Even though her brain told her to close her mouth, her jaw hung open. "You've got to be joking."

He scowled. "Do I look like I'm laughing?"

"This is ridiculous." Feeling cornered, she brushed past him and pressed a hand against the kitchen door. She had more important things to do than argue over something she didn't need to worry about this second.

"I mean it, Josie. No chances." He reached for her elbow.

Her side vision showed Agnes pretending to wipe a table, but Josie knew she hung on to their words. Schooling her tone, she shook her arm free and snapped a salute. "Aye aye, captain. Now if you will excuse me, I need to get to work. Unless you have something to say about that, too."

Nick glared at her, then spun on his heel and slammed out the front door. "What is his problem?"

"He looked madder than a porcupine with a hangnail." Agnes carried the cleaning supplies back to the kitchen.

For the next two hours, Josie baked, crossing cranberry walnut scones, lemon poppyseed muffins and raspberry cheesecake brownies off her list while trying to tune out Nick's lecture. His disappointment leached into every cell of her body. Being called irresponsible dented her heart, but she wouldn't let him know that.

The timer dinged. She pulled out the raspberry cheese-cake brownies and set them on the stove. Flipping off the oven, she glared at the clock and headed for the dining room to find Agnes.

"Agnes, I need to run my car over to the garage and drop it off to get the tire fixed before Nick has a cow."

Agnes erased the breakfast specials from the whiteboard and added the lunch special—white chicken chili. "He has your best interests at heart, Sugar Pie."

Josie snorted. "He's acted like a dictator, coming in with guns blazing. It's not like we're married or anything. And that spare is perfectly safe. I'll drop it off and walk back. See you in about half an hour."

She headed for her office, grabbed her wool coat and purse from her office, and stepped out the back door. Keys in hand, she unlocked the car with the remote, then stopped.

Nick Brennan was a dead man.

Her car sported four new tires, black as ink.

She had a business to run. She couldn't drop everything and get her tire fixed because he demanded it. But that gave him no right to interfere again! First her mortgage, now her car.

And what had he done—bribed some mechanic to come and replace the tires on the spot? She had her keys. Unless he'd come in the back door and lifted them from her purse. He wouldn't have dared.

She stormed into her office, flung her purse and keys on the chair, then thundered through the kitchen. Not seeing Agnes, she bolted into the dining room.

Agnes stood behind the counter talking to Walt and the men from his group home.

Josie dialed her anger down to simmer and smiled at them. "Hey, guys."

Paul nodded twice, then took two steps back. Ernie smiled and clutched his doll Fredrick's arm and imitated a wave. Gideon hugged her.

Patting his back, she noticed a new guy standing next to Walt. Something about his dark hair and blue eyes seemed familiar, yet she couldn't put her finger on it. He must be new at Jacob House. But where had she seen him before?

Walt put a hand on the man's shoulder and nodded toward Josie. "Ross, this is Josie. She owns this place. Josie, I'd like you to meet Ross Brennan. He's new at our house."

Brennan?

A chill colder than an Arctic wind blew across Josie's bones. She forced herself not to shiver.

Not Nick's brother? No way.

The Ross she remembered was a gangly kid constantly on the move, usually with a basketball in his hands.

Why hadn't he told her? The first night she talked with Nick, he had said his brother was fine. But now that she thought about it, he did pause before saying Ross was fine. Then when she dropped the extra doughnuts off at Jacob House last month and caught sight of Nick, she meant to ask why he was there, but forgot. Now she knew. A tremor shuddered down her spine.

Her brain numb, she stuck out a hand to shake his. His hand, though warm and soft, felt limp compared to Nick's strong grip. "Nice to meet you, Ross."

"You're the lady in the picture."

"The picture?" She glanced at Walt for clarification.

Walt shrugged, then turned to Ross. "What picture, Ross?"

Ross pulled a camera out of his coat pocket and with shaky fingers, he thumbed through the photos on the display screen. Smiling, he held the camera up for her to see. "This one."

She reached for the camera. The photo she had given Nick that first night, of her and Hannah, lay on a table. Someone had taken a slightly blurry picture of the photograph. "Where did you get this picture, Ross?"

"It was on Super Nick's table."

"Super Nick?"

"Yes, Super Nick is my brother. He's my hero."

She was ready to ring Nick's neck, but now his brother claimed he was a superhero. Why hadn't he told her about Ross? Was he embarrassed about his brother's condition? Did that mean he was embarrassed about having a sick daughter, too? What other secrets was he keeping from her?

Nick didn't deserve this beautiful little girl with peach fuzz for hair, circles under her eyes as dark as dusk and milky skin.

Or the furnished apartment with the white walls, natural wood trim and large windows that allowed the midmorning sun to spill across the beige carpet. Not to mention the incredible scents that drifted up from the shop below. The air in the hall smelled like cookies and something chocolate.

Once the contractor finished the bathroom, Josie offered him the use of the apartment above the coffee shop. He appreciated not having to camp out at the Holiday Inn, but insisted on paying rent. Hanging on to his apartment in Linwood Park drained his savings account faster than he would have liked, but being in Shelby Lake with Ross, Hannah and Josie was more important.

He needed to be here for Hannah and Josie. At least the stubborn woman allowed him to tutor Hannah. No sense in paying for someone when he was more than qualified to help their daughter stay on top of her schoolwork at her own pace. They completed today's assignments and relaxed with a rousing game of Go Fish.

Watching Hannah ponder her cards, the way her nose wrinkled as she thought out her strategy, filled Nick with an emotion he was afraid to label. He felt as if someone had given him a special pass to Disney World, and it was almost closing time. He swallowed the knot in his throat. He had no idea how to be a dad. Josie didn't hand him a parenting manual. He didn't have the most stellar example in his own dad. Right now, he was winging it and praying he didn't screw up too badly.

"Earth to Dad." Hannah snapped her fingers in front of his face.

He blinked several times. "Sorry, I was lost in thought."

"Does your mental GPS need recalibrating?" She pushed up the brim of her floppy denim hat and charmed him to the core with her lopsided grin.

"I'm impressed. Where'd you learn such a big word?"

"Please. I'm not a baby. Do you have any eights?"

Nick glanced down at the three cards in his hand—two eights and a four. He flicked the two requested cards across the couch cushion. They landed on top of her purple fleece blanket. "You're creaming me."

She gave him that lopsided grin again. "That's the point." She scooped up the two cards, added her own and then put them on the growing pile of matches in front of her. "I'm out."

"You win again. What's that—four to three?"

"Yep, I won the tiebreaker. Want to play again?" Hannah turned her cards over and pushed them together in a pile. She leaned back against the couch and closed her eyes for a second.

His heart twisted. As soon as her team at the children's hospital decided she was ready to begin the transplant process, he'd have his cells harvested and they could proceed with the next step. Until then, they had to keep her as healthy as possible.

"How about a break? I don't think my brain can handle trying to come up with more strategies." Nick gathered the cards and shuffled the deck. He wrapped a rubber band around them, and tossed them on the coffee table. "You're quite the cardsharp. Who taught you to play so well?"

"Michelle—one of the nurses at the hospital. When you're there, like, forever, games keep you from getting bored to death."

"Are there a lot of kids when you're in the hospital?" Nick moved to Hannah's end of the couch. He leaned her forward, plumped her pillow and then pressed her back against it. She rested her legs in his lap, settled into the pillow and sighed, her breathing sounding more labored than usual.

"Not a lot. Some come in for quick trips like operations. Some stay longer because they're sick like me." She reached for his hand.

"That must be tough." He ran a thumb over her narrow fingers. Pretty hands like her mother's.

"It was at first, especially on days when Mom couldn't be there. The nurses are really nice. Michelle is my favorite one. She has pretty brown hair and a nice smile. She tells us stories about Louie the alien." Hannah's eyes twinkled as she bit down on her bottom lip.

Nick raised his eyebrows and shot her an "are you serious" look. "Louie the alien?"

"Yep. He lives in the children's ward and eats the green Jell-O that the kids don't like."

"Have you met Louie?"

She giggled. "No, silly. He comes out only at night when we're sleeping. He leaves us green treats, too."

"Like what?"

"Sherbet. Cupcakes with green frosting. Green apples. Green popcorn balls. Green grapes." Hannah yawned, her eyelashes fluttering closed.

"What's the hardest part about being in the hospital?"

He needed to shut up so she could sleep, but his curiosity demanded satisfaction.

"Missing my family and my friends. Sometimes my friends can't visit because of germs. But lately only Ashley has been coming to see me. I guess they think I'm a weirdo or something." The light in her eyes faded. She picked at the seam of her blanket.

Nick ran his thumb across her cheek. "You know, sweetheart, I think it's more like they don't know what to say or how to act."

"Yeah, but I'm still the same." She struggled to sit up.

"Your friends might not understand what's happening to your body. You're still the same person on the inside, but your outside is changing a little. That may scare them."

"See, I told you I was a freak."

Nick tapped the end of her nose. "And what did I say about calling yourself a freak?"

"To stop it." Her bottom lip plumped out.

"I'm sure your friends miss hanging out with you, too. Maybe they have questions, but don't want to upset you by asking them."

"How do you know?"

He couldn't tell her about Ross. Not yet. He needed more time to strengthen their relationship before he dropped the bomb about destroying his family.

"I have…this friend who was in a bad car accident. He was a star basketball player with lots of friends. His brain was injured in that accident, and that changed the way he talked and acted. Many of his friends didn't know what to say or how to act, so they just stopped visiting altogether. Now he has a new circle of friends who like him inside and out."

"I would be his friend."

"I know you would, sweetheart. So how about closing your eyes and getting some rest?"

"Can we take a walk instead? Maybe go to the park?"

"Grab your coat. Let's see if your mom is ready for a break. Maybe she'll walk with us."

Once they shrugged into their coats and Hannah adjusted her hat, they headed downstairs and stepped outside.

Tiny green buds dotted the tree limbs. Patches of green appeared beneath melting snow. Puffs of their breath reminded them of the sun's deception.

"The sun was warm but the wind was chill. You know how it is with an April day,'" Nick said.

"Did you just make that up?" Hannah hunched her shoulders against the chill.

"Not unless my name is Robert Frost."

"Nice try with that one. Mom said you were the editor of the school paper when you were in high school. Do you still write?"

Nick held the Cuppa Josie's door open for her. "Academic papers. Nothing worth mentioning."

She paused in the doorway and looked up at him. "Mom said you used to write poetry."

"Your mom talks too much."

"I'm going to tell her you said that."

"So what will it take to buy your silence?"

"Are you bribing me?"

"Quite possibly."

"How about some hot chocolate?"

"You drive a hard bargain." He ushered her into the shop and out of the chilly air. The bells rattled against the glass as the door closed.

A group of guys gathered near the register. One of them turned and a wide smile spread across his face. "Super Nick!"

Nick's blood ran cold. His gaze connected with Josie's. The look of hurt that glimmered in her eyes told him his two worlds had just collided. And it would take some serious damage control to put the wreckage back together.

Chapter Eleven

Josie poured milk into the metal pitcher, filling it halfway, and tried not to slosh it over the side. With the way her hands shook, it was a feat for a task she could normally do in her sleep.

Focus, girl. One step at a time.

Purge the steam arm. Stretch the milk. Texturize it. Thinking through the steps drowned out the unspoken words clanging inside her head.

Bubbles climbed the sides of the pitcher. The metal warmed in her hand. She turned off the knob and set the milk on the hot mat next to the machine. Grabbing a clean cloth, she wiped the steam arm.

She added a squirt of dark chocolate, followed by a shot of vanilla syrup, into a stout café mug, stirred in the steamed milk and added a mound of her homemade whipped cream.

The same question rolled around in her head for the four-hundredth time—why didn't Nick tell her about Ross?

Blinking away the pressure building behind her eyes, she grabbed a spoon and carried the hot chocolate to the corner table where Hannah sat chatting with her dad.

Nick shifted to his feet when she approached. "Josie…"

"Don't." She set the hot chocolate on the table, wiped her hand on her apron and kissed the top of Hannah's head. "There you go, sweetie."

Hannah smiled up at her, blissfully unaware of the current of tension rippling between her parents. "Thanks, Mom."

Ignoring Nick's pleading eyes, she returned to the counter to clean up her mess. Spying the empty milk jug, she carried it into the kitchen and tossed it into the sink to be rinsed before going into the recycling bin.

Gripping the refrigerator handle, she pressed her forehead against the cool stainless-steel door. What was the big deal? So he didn't tell her about what happened with Ross. Was it really any of her business? Still, her heart ached from his lack of trust in her.

"Josie."

She pulled fresh milk from the fridge and turned to find Nick leaning a shoulder against the doorjamb, blocking her exit. Escaping through the back door and circling around the building to the front seemed a bit childish. But she pondered it. For a minute.

"We need to talk."

"It will have to wait. I have work to do." She attempted to brush past him, but he caught her arm.

His eyes begged her to listen. "At least give me a minute to explain—"

"Explain what, Nick?" Josie clutched the cold gallon to her chest, hoping it would soothe her throbbing heart. Her eyes burned. She wouldn't fall apart in front of him. "That you don't trust me enough to know about your brother?"

His shoulders slumped. "Trust has nothing to do with it."

She wanted to believe him. With all her heart. But she couldn't shake the fear that their relationship was more one-sided than she wanted to admit. "Could have fooled me."

He rubbed a thumb and forefinger over his eyelids. "It's not you, Josie. It's...complicated."

Josie rolled her eyes. "You don't think I can handle complicated, Professor?"

He crossed his arms over his chest, feet shoulder width apart and a scowl etched his forehead. "Knock it off. That's not what I meant and you know it."

"No, I don't, because you haven't shared anything with me." Maybe she had been imagining everything that had been happening between them—the near kiss, trips down memory lane, the looks that made her stomach flip over. He was here for Hannah. She was an idiot to think anything could happen between them again. Once he honored his promise to help Hannah, he'd be out of their lives and she'd be back to shouldering everything by herself.

Nick rubbed a finger over his earlobe. "I said this has nothing to do with you. Come upstairs and give me a chance to explain."

He dropped onto the hunter-green couch left behind by the previous renter and cradled his head in his hands. What a mess. How was he going to put these pieces back together? An ache throbbed at the base of his skull. He rolled his neck to ease knots of tension.

Spying a stray Go Fish card sticking out from under the couch, he picked it up and tossed it in the end table drawer with the rest.

Josie took Hannah home to stay with *Nonno*, but promised to come back so they could talk. Hopefully by then he'd be able to string some words together so she could understand it had nothing to do with her.

He stood and grabbed their empty glasses to carry them

to the sink. He returned to the living room and folded Hannah's blanket, placing it on her backpack by the door.

He appreciated the apartment, but the empty walls and bare furnishings didn't scream welcoming and cozy the way Josie's did. Instead, it screamed temporary, good enough for now, limbo. Was that how Josie saw their relationship?

A knock on the door echoed off the plain walls. About time.

He stalked to the door, opened it then stood back so Josie could enter.

She'd changed before coming back, replacing her brown work pants and blue shirt with jeans and a black turtleneck sweater that emphasized the milky whiteness of her skin. Her hair, free from her usual clip, curled down her back.

"Come in."

Josie brushed past him. "This had better be good."

He crossed the door and swallowed a groan.

She whirled around and faced him, eyes blazing. "I trusted you with the most precious person in my life, and you haven't trusted me with anything."

She didn't waste any time in nailing him to the wall.

"It's not that simple." Nick walked across the room to the window, rubbing his hand over the back of his neck before turning to face her. "I can explain."

"What's to explain? You don't trust me." She pulled her jacket tighter around herself.

Nick held out his hands, palms up. "What did you expect me to do, Josie? Waltz into your living room that first night and say, 'Oh, by the way, my brother has brain damage because of me.' Yeah, I would have scored high on the confidence meter."

Josie planted a hand on her hip. "Don't make me out to be the bad guy. You've had plenty of chances since then."

"You're the one with trust issues. You got bent out of shape when I helped you out. You've been holding me at arm's length since you pulled my picture off the wall."

"You went behind my back, Nick. Those aren't exactly trust builders. I couldn't drop everything at work to get my tire fixed. But that wasn't good enough. You had to ride in on your white steed and save the day." She strode to the window and poked him in the chest.

Nick grabbed her shoulders and gave her a gentle shake. "I didn't want anything to happen to you, okay? I couldn't lose you, too, Josie. And if I could fix it I would. I'm not going to apologize for helping you out." He dropped his hands and pinched the bridge of his nose. "Look, I don't want to fight about this."

She stepped back and dropped on the ugly armchair with the saggy cushion and reached for the frayed throw pillow, clutching it to her chest. "So if it's not about trust, then why all the secrecy?"

Scrubbing a hand over his face, Nick exhaled. He moved away from the window and slumped on the couch. "Like I said downstairs—this has nothing to do with you. I wanted time to get to know Hannah without complicating the relationship by pulling my family into it. I was afraid once you learned the truth, you wouldn't want me around anymore."

Josie shrugged out of her coat and laid it across the back of the chair. "Friends trust one another. You didn't give me a chance to make a choice."

"I trust you, okay?"

"Then tell me about Ross."

Nick rubbed his forehead, his stomach tightening with each second that passed. He blew out a breath. "Just so you know, what I tell you could change everything."

"What do you mean?" She frowned.

"Like I said, you may not want me around Hannah anymore." Unable to sit still, Nick jumped to his feet and paced.

"Let me be the judge of that."

Moving back to the window, he stared at the pavement below, clear and warmed by the late-afternoon sun. He squeezed his eyes shut, remembering another pavement, the moon reflecting off the ice. "Eight years ago, I came home for Ross's basketball championship game during his senior year in high school. Ten seconds left on the clock, and Ross scored a seemingly impossible shot, taking his team to victory."

"You must've been thrilled."

Nick opened his eyes and glanced at her over his shoulder. "Definitely. Ross bounced on adrenaline. He asked me to give him a lift to Maria's Pizza—remember that place on the corner of Eighth and Grant?" Seeing Josie's nod, he continued, "The team was going to hang out there to celebrate. I planned to drop off Ross, then Mom and I were heading back to her house." His heartbeat stumbled. "It snowed during the game. If only I had paid more attention to the roads instead of going on with Ross about his winning shot."

Nick swallowed a lump in his throat and rubbed a hand under his nose. The street below blurred. He felt Josie move behind him before he saw her in his peripheral vision.

She placed a gentle hand on his shoulder. "What happened?"

His chest heaved. He pulled in a deep breath. No going back. She needed to know the truth. For Hannah's sake.

"I hit a patch of black ice before the stoplight, slid out of control and into the path of a half-ton pickup turning left."

"Oh, Nick." Her voice broke.

He didn't want her pity. He didn't deserve it.

"Mom...Mom died instantly." He rubbed a hand over his eyes, clearing his vision. "Ross spent weeks in the ICU, then surgeries and therapies. If only I had seen the ice..." Tears burned his eyes. His jaw quivered.

Josie pulled him toward her and wrapped her arms around him. "I'm so sorry, Nick. So so sorry. It was an accident. Not your fault."

"My mom, Josie. She's dead because of me." He crushed her to his chest, burying his face in her shoulder. His fingers twined in her hair. His chest quaked. Shadows from the past crashed through his head like bumper cars. His fists clenched as he remembered the feel of his beater sliding on the ice. His mother's screaming and Ross's shouts echoed in his ears. The whine of tires, the sickening crunch of metal on metal, the stench of gasoline, the sticky feel of Ross's blood on his hands when he tried to find his brother's pulse, the vacant look in his mother's eyes.

He blinked away the ghostly images. Nothing could dissolve the nauseating taste of regret that coated the back of his throat. He was the one driving. What he had done was unforgivable. And knowing the truth, there was no way Josie would trust him with Hannah. His dream of a family evaporated like the morning fog.

Chapter Twelve

Josie flipped her pillow and bunched it beneath her neck. A glance at the clock showed it to be 1:26 a.m.

Every time she closed her eyes, Nick's anguished face haunted her. They stood near that window in his apartment just twelve hours ago crying together. Of course, he was embarrassed by his breakdown, but she didn't mind. She couldn't imagine carrying around such a heavy burden. She spent another hour reassuring him that as far as Hannah was concerned nothing between them had swelled.

She had ranted about trust, making it all about her.

Dear Lord, please guard and protect his heart. Allow him to feel Your comforting presence.

With sleep being a stranger, maybe a cup of hot tea would help. Josie flung the blankets aside and moved out of bed, reaching for her bathrobe lying across the cedar chest at the end of her bed.

"Mom!"

Josie dropped the bathrobe and raced down the hall. She flipped on Hannah's bedroom light. "Hannah? What's wrong?"

Half sitting and wide-eyed, Hannah's hands twisted in the sheets, her breathing coming in tight wheezes.

Josie checked the white nightstand for Hannah's medicine. "Where's your inhaler?"

Hannah shook her head.

Josie opened the drawer and rummaged inside. Not finding it, she dropped to her hands and knees to check the floor and ran a hand across the carpet. The whistling sound in her daughter's chest forced Josie to move faster. The inhaler lay under the bed.

She stretched, but couldn't quite reach it. She pressed her shoulder against Hannah's bed frame and heaved with all of her might. The bed shifted about two inches, which was enough for Josie to reach the medicine. As she scooted out from under the bed and sat up, she rapped her head on the open drawer of Hannah's nightstand. Pain exploded across her skull. She fought back tears and clamped down to prevent screaming out the words that blistered her tongue.

She shook the inhaler and handed it to Hannah, who took two quick puffs.

Josie held her breath and counted in her head. One, two, three, four, five. Time passed in slow motion.

Within seconds, Hannah's breathing regulated—each breath a relief and the beginning of fear. She hadn't had an attack in a while. Would there be another tonight? Time was the enemy.

"You okay, sweetie?"

"My chest hurts. Can I have some water?"

Still rubbing the sore spot on her head, Josie headed to the bathroom. Her hand shook as she filled a glass with water. What if she had been sleeping? Would she have heard Hannah cry out?

She carried the water to Hannah, who drank it and

handed her the empty glass. Josie set it on the nightstand and sat on the bed beside Hannah. She cradled Hannah against her chest, still not liking the sound of her breathing. "I need to call Dr. Kym and let her know about your attack."

Hannah tightened her grip on Josie. "No, don't go. Stay with me."

Josie started to sit up and untangle herself. "I'll be right back."

"Please, Mommy." The plea in Hannah's voice caused her to sag back against the pillows.

Josie sighed. She rubbed a hand over Hannah's head and kissed her forehead. "Okay, I'll stay, but I'm calling her if you get worse."

Josie drew Hannah close and rubbed her back. She hated being able to feel her daughter's bones and the uncertainty that hovered like a cloud.

Lord, give her breath. Give her strength.

Her throat thickened. She squeezed her eyes shut and sucked in her lips.

"Tonight was Ashley's slumber party."

Josie reached over and flicked on the candlestick lamp on Hannah's nightstand. They winced at the bright light. She tilted Hannah's chin to meet her gaze. "Oh, honey. Why didn't you say something?"

Shrugging, Hannah rested her head against Josie's shoulder. "I emailed her and said I didn't feel like coming."

"Why not? You were so excited to go."

"I don't know. Ashley kept talking about these purple feather extensions her mom bought to put in our hair."

"Kind of hard to add extensions to these cute little wisps, huh?" Josie fingered the fringes around Hannah's ears.

"Yeah, just a little. I hate looking like a freak." Hannah traced one of the printed daisies on her comforter.

Josie tilted Hannah's chin up. "You have to stop using that word. You are far from looking like a freak. You are a beautiful girl."

"That's easy for you to say. You're my mom. You took an oath or something to say nice things about me." Hannah twirled one of Josie's curls around her fingers. "Plus, you have all of this gorgeous hair. How would you feel if you lost it all?"

A rush of wetness blurred Josie's tired eyes. "Oh, Hannah, if I could, I'd trade places with you faster than you could blink."

Josie cradled Hannah and rocked her until she felt her daughter's breathing even out and become more rhythmic. Once she was sure Hannah was asleep, she laid her back on the pillow and tucked the purple-and-white daisy comforter around her. She pulled her arm away.

"Don't go," Hannah mumbled, her eyes still closed.

"I'm not going anywhere." Josie slid an arm back under here for you, baby. Always." She closed her eyes for a second, an idea forming how she could help Hannah feel less self-conscious.

Shards of light fractured the shadows. Nick clawed his way out of the abyss of the nightmare that held his sub-conscious hostage. Heart pounding, he forced his eyes open and gulped in air to loosen the constrictive bands around his chest.

He wiped a shaky hand over his sweat-soaked face. The water. The collapsing bridge. Hannah.

Oh, dear God. He lost Hannah.

Bile scorched the back of his throat.

Nick kicked his legs free of the twisted blankets and

sat on the edge of the bed, cradling his head in his hands. He lost Hannah.

No, he didn't. She was fine. It was just a dream.

It seemed so real.

Hannah was safe.

If he closed his eyes, he could still see the distorted images through the car windshield in his dream.

The stone bridge without guardrails provided his only course of crossing over the rising river. Turning back wasn't an option. He had to move forward. Once the car was in the middle of the bridge, the water raged against the doors, soaking the interior. He peered through the windshield again to see his daughter being swept over the side of the bridge. Where had she come from?

Josie threw herself in front of his car, begging him to save her daughter. His mother sat in the passenger seat, urging him to keep going across the bridge.

But he couldn't. He couldn't leave his daughter. He had to save her.

Abandoning the vehicle, he charged through the rising water and grabbed Hannah's hands. He begged her to hold on, not to let go, but she cried out about it hurting too much. Her tiny fingers slipped out of his grasp.

He woke himself up by screaming her name.

Breathing hard, his chest shuddered as he tried to force his heart to slow.

Only a dream. His daughter was safe.

He didn't need to lie on some shrink's couch to figure out the symbolism of the nightmare. Stress had a way of messing with a guy's mind, especially after reliving the accident with Josie and bawling like a baby.

He'd dropped into bed like a stone and slept until he'd had to force himself awake.

Stumbling to the window, he jerked open the curtain

and pushed up the window, letting the crisp air cool his clammy skin. Shelby Lake residents slept as he untangled his mind from the horrific images that replayed in his head.

The stillness of the inky lake against the dawning horizon beckoned with its wide spaces and open air.

He closed the window and rummaged through his dresser for running clothes. He threw on shorts and a Linwood Park sweatshirt and then jammed his feet into his running shoes. Grabbing his wallet and keys, he headed out the door.

Throwing himself behind the wheel, he started the engine and backed out of the parking space. He drove down Center Street until he reached the turnoff for the lake, passing only a car or two. After parking in the empty beach lot, he jogged the short stretch to the dirt path that snaked along the lake and started off with a light jog to warm his tight muscles.

How long had it been since he'd run? A week? Maybe two? He couldn't remember. But the rush of freedom warmed his joints as his shoes scuffed against the dirt path. One foot in front of the other. Measured breaths filled his lungs. The chilly air stroked his cheeks. He should've grabbed a hat. Too late now.

The earthy scent of April rains mingled with decayed leaves left over from last fall. Birds twittered in the budding branches above his head. An explosion of hot pink and melted gold pushed away the night as the sun stretched over the hilltops and reflected off the glassy lake. Mist arose from the water.

A bullfrog croaked as his footfalls added to nature's symphony. A family of ducks waddled across the path in front of him. He stopped, jogging in place and watched the ducklings follow their mother into the water.

A stitch in his side caused his steps to slow. His muscles

burned. He should've grabbed a bottle of water on his way out the door, but running to chase away the night's demons had been his only concern.

He needed to shower and then head over to Josie's to see if there were any lingering effects from yesterday's talk. And he needed to see with his own eyes that they were fine. He wouldn't lose his daughter—no matter what it took to save her.

Chapter Thirteen

If Josie could be granted three wishes, one of them would be that she wasn't allergic to caffeine. She could use the extra jolt right about now. Her gritty eyelids burned and felt as if they weighed half a ton.

Smothering a yawn, she poured hot water over her tea bag and set the kettle back on the stove. Like a genie, the scent of vanilla rose and tickled her nose.

A quick glance at her phone showed Nick still hadn't phoned. She'd called after Hannah finally fell asleep, but Nick must not have heard the phone.

Stretching out next to Hannah in her twin bed hadn't done Josie's knotted muscles any favors. And getting less than three hours' sleep hadn't helped, either. At least she had peace of mind that Hannah's breathing had returned to normal.

She sat at the island to read today's devotional focused on one of her favorite verses from Romans.

May the God of hope fill you with all joy and peace as you trust in Him, so that you may overflow with hope by the power of the Holy Spirit.

She wasn't doing so well in the trust department these days. And that was stealing her joy. The physical exhaustion that weighed her down was nothing compared to the mental fatigue that battered her hope and peace.

The back door that led into the kitchen opened. Lindsey knocked on the door frame and peeked her head inside.

"Hey, you. Mind if I come in?"

Josie looked up and waved her in, trying not to covet her stepsister's radiant face fresh from a full night's sleep.

"Hey, I was just making tea. Want some?"

"Sure. That would be great." Lindsey set her purse on the table and shrugged out of her coat. Static from her jacket caused her long honey-blond hair to flare out. Her pink cardigan sweater highlighted the glow on her face.

"What are you doing out so early?" Josie padded to the cabinet and reached for another mug.

Lindsey smoothed down her hair, and then took the mug from Josie. She reached into the canister on the counter for a tea bag. "I had to take Tyler to school and dropped by the shop, but Agnes said you called in sick. Everything okay?"

"Hannah had an asthma attack last night. Probably stress related, but I need to call the doctor in case something else is wrong. And with no sleep, I'd be biting off heads." She didn't mention anything about Nick. That wasn't her story to tell.

"Sweetie, I'm sorry. I totally get the head biting thing." She caressed the barely visible bump. "My hormones are so out of whack, poor Stephen is going to start calling me Dr. Jekyll and Mrs. Hyde."

Josie eyed her stepsister's baby bump. "You have an excuse."

"And you don't? Oh, girl, everyone totally understands. I simply can't imagine what you're going through." Lindsey set the mug next to the stove and pulled Josie into a hug.

Blinking back tears, Josie mumbled into Lindsey's

shoulders. "I hate being such a wimp. Sometimes I think Hannah's handling everything better than I am. Besides, you've gone through your own share of trials. Look at you now."

"You're one of the strongest women I know, Josie. So far from being a wimp." She drew back to look at Josie. "Besides, I had to learn with God on my side, how can I go wrong?"

Josie rubbed the heel of her hand over her eyes, pulled out one of the island stools for Lindsey and sat on the other. "Did you ever wonder if God heard your prayers?"

Reaching for her mug, Lindsey sat on the other stool. She dunked her tea bag. "Like almost every day after Dad died and Stephen married Bethany. But God won't leave you, no matter how tough your circumstances may seem."

"I know that. I do. My head and my heart seem to be on different planets right now, though. Sometimes I just get so angry. Why Hannah?" Josie glanced at the clock above the sink. "But enough of this pity party. Since you're here, could you do me a huge favor?"

"Anything. You know that."

"I need to run an errand. It'll take less than an hour. Will you stay with Hannah? She's still asleep."

"No problem. Take all the time you need. I'll give Stephen a call and let him know where I am."

"You two are so cute. It makes me sick." Josie smiled to show she was kidding.

"Your man is out there." Lindsey winked. "Even closer than you may think."

After hearing Nick's story yesterday, Josie's hope for a future with him had evaporated. He had enough on his plate already with Ross. And they were just too different now. Besides, he hadn't even asked or hinted.

"Don't hold your breath."

* * *

I am not going to cry. Hannah, this is for you, baby.

Josie sat in the stylist's chair at Shear Pleasure and closed her eyes to keep from staring at the bits of hair on the black-and-white-tiled floor.

"Okay, I'm going to turn you around now so you can see for yourself." Natalie, Josie's stylist, swiveled her around and removed the pink-and-white-striped polyester cape, setting it on the gray marble counter littered with styling tools.

Josie stared at her reflection in the mirror hanging over Natalie's station. Her breath caught in her throat. She didn't think getting her hair cut would leave her feeling so... vulnerable. Hannah had asked how she would feel with no hair.

"Check out the back." Natalie handed her a large mirror and turned the chair again.

Josie positioned the mirror to see the back of her head. She stroked the nape of her neck, feeling very exposed. Vulnerable. Naked.

She handed the mirror back to Natalie and cracked a smile. "Thanks, Nat."

"New cuts can be a shock at first, but you'll get used to it. Your facial structure is perfect for this cut. I wouldn't steer you wrong." Natalie handed Josie a baggie filled with a coiled ponytail. "Here you go."

Josie withdrew a long thick ponytail held together by a rubber band. What used to be attached to her head. All fourteen inches of it. Returning it to the bag, she stood and brushed a stray piece of hair from her shirt. "Thanks for opening up early for me, Natalie."

Natalie slid her trendy black-framed glasses to the top of her head, using them to hold her caramel-highlighted hair away from her face. "Anything for you, honey. And remember, it's only hair. You've done a great thing."

In her heart, she knew she made the right decision. After all, she'd do anything for Hannah. For the first time since Hannah's chemo caused her hair loss, Josie had a slight understanding of how her daughter felt.

Of course, she wasn't totally bald, or even close.

But after having long curls for most of her life, the pixie cut would take time to get used to. Natalie had added a little mousse for body on top and swept her longish bangs to the side. She hadn't had bangs since high school, but she trusted Natalie to work her scissor magic. She dropped the ponytail into her purse the same time her phone rang. She fished it out. Nick's number appeared in the display.

"Nick." Josie gathered her coat off the adjacent stylist chair.

"Josie, I'm sorry I didn't get your call before this. I went for a run."

She rubbed a hand over her forehead, longing for a nap. "No worries. You okay?"

"Yeah, I'm fine. How about you? Your voice sounds funny."

"I'm tired. Didn't get much sleep." She shouldered her phone while she dug a twenty out of her wallet and handed it to Natalie. She waved away the five in Natalie's hand and mouthed for her to keep it.

Heading out the door into the brisk cold, she flipped up the collar to protect her naked neck from the wind and told Nick about Hannah's rough night. She decided not to tell him where she was or what she had done. He'd find out soon enough.

When they had dated, he always commented on how pretty her hair was. Would he still think the same? Did she care? Probably more than she should.

* * *

After hearing about his daughter's night, Nick's heart weighed like a cannonball in his chest. The fatigue in Josie's voice made him wish he had been there to help with Hannah.

Man, the past few weeks… He scratched the back of his head and blew out a breath.

He needed to do something for Hannah. And for Josie. To show both of them how much they meant to him.

An hour later, after a quick stop at Winston's Barber Shop, he pulled into Josie's driveway. Shifting his truck into Park, he stared at the Disney-like cottage with its crazy fairy door knocker. Could he see himself living here? Mowing the yard? Shoveling snow? Pushing Hannah on the swing hanging from the sturdy oak in the backyard? Most definitely.

The more he was around Josie, the harder he kicked himself for letting her go a decade ago. What if they had stayed together? He wouldn't have missed all those milestones in Hannah's life. He could have partnered with Josie for this parenting gig.

What did Josie say last night? Regrets couldn't turn back the clock. He needed to learn his lessons from those life experiences and push forward. Even if his current situation seemed more like a dance routine with two steps forward and one step back?

Shutting off the engine, he slid out from behind the wheel. As he headed to the front door, his heart raced the way it did the night he picked up Josie for their first date all those years ago—pizza and a movie.

He couldn't remember what movie they saw or their pizza toppings, but he remembered wanting to release her hair from the ponytail she wore and smell the fruity scent of her shampoo. That night he fell head over heels in love with the shy girl who dreamed of traveling the world and journaling her experience. Because of him, she didn't make it out of the state.

He rubbed a hand over the back of his head, still not used to the lack of hair. He jammed his thumb in the doorbell. Would Josie think he was an idiot? Really, what would a haircut prove, anyway? Maybe he was an idiot, but it was too late now.

Hannah opened the door, wearing her flowered floppy hat, a yellow long-sleeved T-shirt with a frog on the front that held a sign that read Toadly Awesome, jeans and striped socks. "Dad!"

He knelt, pressing one denim-covered knee to the welcome mat and opened his arms.

Hannah wrapped her arms around his neck. He breathed in the scent of her soap—the same clean scent Josie used—and tried not to notice the way her shirt hung on her tiny frame or listen to her labored breathing. His chest tightened. He never wanted to let go.

Her head came up, knocking back the brim of his hat. She reached up to straighten it and then jerked it off his head. Her mouth dropped open. She clapped a hand over her lips, but it wasn't quick enough to muffle the giggle—a sound that was music to his ears. "Wait until Mom sees you. You're made for each other."

He could only hope.

Chapter Fourteen

One of Josie's favorite memories as a child was making *zeppole*—pastrylike fluffy doughnuts—with her Italian grandparents.

Josie's great-grandmother had added a special ingredient that set her *zeppole* apart from everyone else's—a secret she shared with *Nonna*, who in turn shared it with Josie.

Now that Hannah had started cooking, Josie shared the family's secret recipe with her.

Would Hannah have a chance to share it with her own family?

Don't even go there, girl.

Josie baked them only at home and didn't offer them in the shop. Every time she bit into one, she was reminded of *Nonna*.

Nonna's voice, scolding *Nonno* for overcooking the dough and getting flour everywhere, crept into her thoughts. *Nonno* would simply kiss her cheek, whisper Italian endearments in her ear and grab the broom.

Josie hoped to have a marriage as strong as theirs. Someday.

She removed the cooked dough from the stove and

scraped it into her stand-up mixer with a heavy wooden spoon.

"Mom, Dad's here."

Josie looked over her shoulder to see Hannah pulling Nick into the kitchen. She glanced at him, then did a double take. The wooden spoon fell against the granite countertop. "Nick, your hair."

Nick gave her a sheepish grin as he scrubbed a hand over his bare scalp. The hair she had loved so much and dreamed about running her hands through—yes, she was finally being honest with herself—was gone. He looked as if he had sat in the barber's chair at boot camp.

"Dad shaved his head for me. Isn't that like the coolest thing ever?"

Josie bit the corner of her lower lip and nodded. Words escaped her. What could she say? "Thank you" seemed so insignificant for the gift he had given Hannah.

A blush stained Nick's cheeks. He shrugged. "No big deal."

Oh, but it was. At least to her. And definitely to Hannah, judging by the mile-wide smile crossing her daughter's face.

Before she could think about what she was doing, Josie rounded the side of the island and wrapped her arms around him. "Thank you."

Nick ran a hand over her head, but stopped at the base of her neck. He turned her around. "Your hair. It's gone, too." She dropped her gaze to her bare feet. "I, uh, got it cut this morning."

He tipped up her chin. "Great minds, huh?"

Josie nodded and searched his face for his reaction.

Nick trailed his fingers gently down the sides of her neck. She resisted a shiver. "Your eyes...man, I didn't think they could get any bigger. That cut makes them look the size of dinner plates. You look great."

She turned back to the mixer so he wouldn't see how his words made her blush like a teenager. "It's a huge change, but totally worth it. My stylist knows a woman who makes wigs for children. Since I wasn't a bone marrow match for Hannah, I figured the least I could do is give her my hair."

Nick wrapped his arms around her waist and rested his chin on the top of her head. "You have a generous heart, June bug. You know that?"

"She's my daughter. I'd give her my life, if that's what it took to make her well again."

"*Our* daughter."

"Right." She whispered, "Our daughter."

Hannah cleared her throat. "Your daughter is right here and about to get sick. Can we get back to making *zeppole*, or are you two still making googly eyes at each other?"

Josie stepped away from Nick and ran her hands down the front of her apron. When he was around, she forgot about everyone else. And that wasn't necessarily a good thing. She cracked an egg, added it to the batter and flipped on the mixer.

If she and Nick could make it work, he'd be there for Hannah, and he wouldn't have to care for Ross all on his own. But was that what he wanted? Josie needed to find out before he spent much more time with them.

"So what are you making?" He leaned on the counter next to her. His closeness, the scent of his soap and the way his collar slid to expose the hollow of his neck forced Josie to keep her eyes on her batter. Not that she wanted to, but it was for the best. For everyone.

She added the rest of the eggs. "*Zeppole.* An Italian pastrylike doughnut. I'm using my *nonna*'s secret recipe."

"What makes it so secret?"

Why did he have to look at her like that? "H-her special ingredient."

"Which is?"

"Uh-uh." She wagged a finger. "Sorry, family secret."

"Aren't I considered family...sort of?" He reached up and brushed a thumb across her cheekbone and showed her the white powder. "Flour."

Nick gave her a slow smile that sent a shiver down to her toes. "Maybe we'll have to fix that. All in the name of doughnuts, of course."

"Afraid not." She turned off the mixer to let the dough cool while she lined a baking sheet with parchment paper.

What could she say to that? And even if she had wanted to, her voice seemed lodged in her throat.

She filled her pastry bag with dough. Nick, Josie and Hannah took turns piping the dough onto the lined baking sheet. Hannah showed Nick how to squeeze the dough out of the bag. Their blobs looked out of place next to her practiced mounds, but to her, they were beautiful. Seeing Hannah glow under her father's attention was so worth it.

Fifteen minutes later, rows of puffed pastries cooled on wire racks. They sprinkled some with powdered sugar. Josie helped Hannah add cream then chocolate on the centers.

Josie offered one to Nick. He popped it in his mouth. Closing his eyes, he moaned. "Those are amazing."

Nonna always said the way to a man's heart was through his stomach. Hearing Nick appreciate her baking warmed her heart.

Hannah stifled a yawn. Josie slid an arm around her daughter's sagging shoulders and directed her toward the living room to rest on the couch with a book. The past hour had taxed her energy level, especially after last night.

Hannah grumbled until Nick promised to join her in a few minutes.

Josie put a dozen of the doughnuts in a plastic container and handed it to Nick. "Why don't you take these to Jacob House? The guys might enjoy them."

He flicked the corner of the container with his thumbnail. "Is that a subtle way of saying you want me to leave?"

"What? No. I was just saying because I figured you'd be seeing Ross today." Josie moved to the sink for the dishcloth. "You're welcome to stay as long as you want. I have to clean up this mess and make dinner. Stay and eat with us." She wasn't ready for him to leave. Not yet. Maybe not ever.

"If you're sure—"

"I am." *Gee, Josie, could you say it any faster?* She piled the dirty dishes in the sink and wiped the counters clean.

"Josie. Can I ask you something?" A hint of uncertainty threaded Nick's voice.

"Sure." She opened the refrigerator and removed the container of chicken breasts she had been marinating.

"What we talked about last night—are you sure that doesn't change things? Like how you feel about me?"

Josie's heart raced faster than her mixer motor. Her hands stilled. Moving back to the island, she forced herself to remove the chicken from the plastic container and place the pieces in a baking dish.

Nick came up behind her and clasped her shoulders. "Josie?"

She tensed, and then relaxed slightly as his thumbs worked magic over her tight neck muscles. "I guess...I guess I'm not quite sure what you mean."

"Well, I'd like to think we were moving in a good direction. Then yesterday...listen, I'm sorry again about not telling you about Ross. It's been tough, you know. I feel so responsible. I guess I didn't want you to feel you couldn't trust me with Hannah. I promise I would never do anything to hurt her intentionally."

Good thing he clarified or she may have humiliated herself since apparently they were thinking two different things.

Josie turned. And realized too late she was pinned between the counter and Nick. She cupped his cheek and ran a thumb over the dark circle under his left eye. "I know that, Nick. And don't worry. I do trust you with Hannah. What happened with your mom and Ross was a tragic accident. You can't keep beating yourself up over it."

"I hurt you by not telling you about Ross. I could see it in your face when I walked into the shop. You were as white as flour."

Josie ducked under his arm and washed her hands. "Hearing what happened was a shock, but no worries. I'm a big girl."

"So we're good? I don't want to jeopardize what we have, but now you know I come as a package deal now." What did they have?

The phone rang, but stopped after one ring. Either the caller hung up, or Hannah answered in the living room.

Hannah came into the kitchen, holding the phone. "Mom, Aunt Lindsey called to see if I could come over and watch a new movie with Tyler. She'll pick me up and bring me home before bed. Please say I can go."

"Honey, I don't know. After last night, I'm not so sure it's a good idea for you be away from the house for a while." She didn't want to be an overprotective mom, but what if something happened and Josie wasn't there?

The verse she'd read this morning from Romans reminded her about needing to trust more.

"Please? I promise to take my inhaler and call the minute I don't feel well. Please, Mom. Say yes."

The pleading in Hannah's eyes pierced Josie's heart. She wanted to say yes. "Your dad's here, though. He's staying for dinner."

"I know, but I really want to go. I've wanted to see this movie, like, forever."

Josie turned to Nick. "Do you mind?"

Nick looked almost surprised that she was asking his opinion. "Me? Not at all. Go, sweetheart, enjoy your movie."

Hannah wrapped her arms around both of them. "Thanks, you're the best parents on the planet. I love you both. Aunt Lindsey is going to pick me up in about fifteen minutes. I'll even rest on the couch until she comes. Oh, and I set the table in the dining room for you."

After Hannah retreated to the living room, Josie stared at the pan of pink chicken breasts still sitting on the island.

"That's a lot of chicken for one person."

"I could stay and help you eat it?"

"You'd still want to do that? I figured with Hannah gone…"

"What? That I'd hit the road? She's not the only reason I'm here, June bug. Maybe I could talk you into more *zeppole* for dessert."

That's what Josie was afraid of. Nick had always been able to talk her into anything. And with Hannah gone for the evening, Josie didn't want history repeating itself.

Nick squirted dish soap into the sink and ran hot water. He folded a dish towel in half, laying it on the bottom. Careful not to chip anything, he set the delicate china plates into the hot water.

A smile slid over his face as he remembered the look on

Josie's face when they carried food into the dining room only to find their mischievous daughter had set the table with a lace tablecloth, Josie's grandmother's fine china and white taper candles.

"Nick, what are you doing?" Josie set two crystal water goblets on the counter next to the sink.

"Washing dishes." He sponged off the plate and set it in the other sink to be rinsed.

"Why?"

He raised an eyebrow and shot her a grin. "Why? Well, it's kind of gross, don't you think, to put them away dirty?"

"Why are you answering questions with questions?" She looked so confused that he wanted to lean over and give her a kiss. But that wouldn't do anything to lessen the confusion—for either of them.

"Why are you asking such silly questions?"

"You don't need to be doing dishes."

"You cooked. It's only fair that I clean up. Just say thanks and let me finish."

She sighed and pushed away from the counter. "Thanks. I'll make you some coffee and we can have doughnuts for dessert."

"Music to my ears."

"I have something I want to show you."

Nick washed the white china with tiny purple flowers bordering the edges, rinsed them and set them in the rack to dry.

Behind him, he could hear Josie grinding beans and making coffee. A couple of minutes later, the rich roast scented the kitchen. He quickly washed the other dishes, wiped off the counters and rinsed out the sinks.

"I'm done in here unless you have a secret stash of dishes hidden somewhere." He turned to see Josie pouring hot water over her tea bag.

"Yes, I stash dishes because I hate washing them." Josie made a face and pushed a plate of *zeppole* toward him. "Take these to the living room. I'll bring your coffee in a minute."

Nick carried the plate into the living room. Sitting on the couch, he set the plate on the antique trunk coffee table next to a pink photo album. Was this what Josie wanted to show him?

Josie carried two steaming mugs into the living room. Nick took the one without a tea bag from her. She smiled her thanks and then sat on the couch. "This is Hannah's baby book. Grace and Lindsey helped me finish it last month."

He took the book. "It's heavy."

"Nine years of her life in one book. I had tons of pictures. The hardest part was trying to decide which ones to use. I'm giving this to Hannah for her birthday next week."

"Are you having a party for her?"

"Most definitely. I will always make a big deal out of her birthday."

Nick opened the first page. A baby with a red face and closed eyes lay on a bed of pink. The words *Hannah Elenora Peretti* arched over the top of the photo with her birth date aligned beneath her photo. Pink paper and baby stickers decorated the page. "Elenora? That's your middle name."

"And my *nonna*'s name. I wanted Hannah to have a small part of her."

Nick turned the page and found a photo of Josie wearing a hospital gown and holding a pink bundle smiling at him. "You look so young."

Guilt gnawed at him. He shifted on the couch.

He turned pages as Josie interjected little anecdotes.

Hannah grew before his eyes. Pictures of her smearing food on her face, sleeping, playing, taking her first steps, getting her first haircut, showing off the gap in her front teeth, her first day of school, laughing with her friends, all the way through to recent pictures of her in the hospital.

All documentations of her life. And he'd missed every single one of them.

He swallowed several times to push out the lump in his throat. "It's beautiful, Josie. She's going to love it. Thank you for sharing it with me."

"I figured she and I could work on her teen years someday. If she gets a chance to be a teen." Josie's voice choked on the last word. She traced the booties embossed on the front.

Nick took the album from her and set it on the trunk. He turned and tilted Josie's chin up with his finger. "What's this 'if' stuff? I'm a match, remember?"

"I know. Since Hannah became sick...I know God has a plan for her. I guess I'm afraid His will for her life may be different than mine. I can't lose her, Nick." She closed her eyes, the struggle with her emotions contorting her face.

Not caring about the consequences, Nick pulled her against his chest. He rubbed her back and rested his cheek against her hair. Josie's tears dampened the front of his sweater. His heart felt as if it were splitting in two. He hadn't known Hannah long, but she'd burrowed deep into his heart. He blinked back wetness from his own eyes.

He'd be here for Josie this time. No matter what happened, she wouldn't have to face it alone.

"I have something for you." Josie pulled away, leaving him missing her warmth. She reached for a tissue off the end table, dried her eyes and picked up a smaller book with hearts scattered across the cover. "This is the journal I wrote in while pregnant with Hannah. I had always been able to tell you anything. And well, journaling…it kind of felt like we were still talking. It was the one place where I could be real. You're welcome to read it. If you want. No big deal if you don't. I wrote about my appointments and Hannah's growth. It's not the same as being there, but if you're interested…well, whatever."

"You're babbling."

Her cheeks brightened. She looked away. "I am. Sorry. Just so you know—there's some stuff that's not so nice about you. I was young. I'm giving it to you now and closing the door to the past."

Nick took the journal and leafed through it. The first line on the first page clenched his stomach—*I'm pregnant. My dad's gonna kill me. And Nick is gone. What am I going to do?*

He flipped to the middle of the book and paused. His blood ran cold. He ran his finger down the page, pushing it toward Josie. "Tell me, uh, about this night."

Josie scanned the words. "It's there on the page."

He turned and cupped her cheek. "Tell me about that night."

Josie dropped her gaze to her fingers. "I was six months pregnant with Hannah. I started having pains. Really sharp ones. I tried to call Dad, but he was at a school board meeting and didn't answer his phone. *Nonno* was someplace—I don't remember where. I was scared, but figured I needed to get the pains checked out. I drove to the E.R. in the rain, feeling more alone than ever. I knew at that moment the only person I could rely on was myself."

"I'm sorry I wasn't there for you before, Josie. I can't even imagine. But that's not going to be the case anymore. I'm always going to be here for you. I promise."

"Don't make promises you don't know if you can keep, Nick."

Nick set the journal on the baby album. "We have a shared history of parents walking out on us. Let's keep Hannah from having that in common with us. I will not abandon my family the way my dad did." He cupped her face. "Josie, when I say I will always be there for Hannah, it's a promise I'll keep until the day I die."

Chapter Fifteen

She wanted to believe him. Really, she did. And even though she told Nick she was closing the door to the past, she still couldn't help but feel like his time in Shelby Lake was temporary. After Hannah's bone marrow transplant, would he leave them and head back to his life in Linwood Park? Or would juggling his responsibilities with Ross keep him too busy to worry about Hannah?

Experience had taught her love didn't stick around. Her mother couldn't be bothered to stick around for the long haul. *Nonna's* death proved love didn't stay forever. And when her dad married Grace, well, Josie realized she had only herself to depend on.

But the look of anticipation on Nick's face—well, it tugged on that cord wrapped around her heart that kept it intact. What if his words were true? What if he planned to be around for the long haul? What then? Would she allow herself to fall in love with him again?

Again? Or still?

She couldn't deny it.

Against her better judgment, she was in love with Nick Brennan.

Now what was she going to do? She couldn't exactly

confess something like that. Quickest way to drive the guy away.

She scraped her thumb across his five-o'clock shadow. "Nick, I don't think—"

"Then don't." Nick placed his finger to her lips. "Stop thinking and just be in the moment. I want to kiss you."

She swallowed, drowning in his melted-chocolate eyes. "I, uh, don't think that's such a great idea."

"There you go thinking again." He stroked her cheekbones.

She reached for one of the chenille throw pillows and clutched it to her chest.

Nick pried her arms off the pillow and tossed it over his shoulder where it thunked against the wall. Her eyes darted, searching for something else to hold. Something to put some distance between them. She started to stand.

Nick grabbed her hand and gently pulled her back to the couch. "Josie."

The way he whispered her name caressed her soul. She closed her eyes and breathed in the faint scent of leather and soap tangled in the knitted fibers of his light blue V-neck sweater.

His hands moved along the curves of her neck. She stifled a shiver. Her stomach fluttered. He lowered his head, his lips caressing hers with the barest of touches. Holding her breath, she hesitated for half a second. Her lips parted as he kissed her again and wrapped his arms around her, pulling her closer. This time, there was no uncertainty. She slid her arms around his neck, sinking into his gentle embrace.

Nick pulled away. She pressed a hand against his chest. His heart raced beneath her palm.

She stole a glance at his face. The tenderness in his eyes awoke a feeling of longing for what could be. If she let it.

This wasn't like the tentative kisses he used to give her in high school. This kiss came from a man who knew what he wanted and made no apologies. But he still had the potential to break her heart.

Josie tried to move away, but Nick anchored an arm around her shoulder. "Don't run."

"I wasn't."

"Tell me what you're thinking." The huskiness in his voice sounded like silk over velvet.

How could she tell him she wanted to spend the rest of her life wrapped in his arms? How could she tell him being close to him made her wish she could turn back time for a do-over? How could she tell him loving him made her heart ache so badly she wanted to curl up in a ball until the feeling went away?

She couldn't. She couldn't tell him any of those things because he'd do what he just accused her of doing—running.

She pulled her gaze away and reached for her now-cold cup of tea. She needed something to hold on to so he wouldn't see the way her hands trembled. "We, uh, probably shouldn't have done that."

He leaned back against the couch, one arm still wrapped around her shoulders. "Seemed like a good idea to me."

"It just makes things more complicated." She shifted away from his arm. She couldn't think when his fingers moved over her skin.

Nick glanced at her, but she couldn't hold his gaze. He blew out a long breath and shifted until both feet hit the floor. He rested his elbows on his knees. "How do you figure?"

"Nick, I have a lot on my plate right now. When you're around, I tend to forget about everything else."

He grinned and waggled his eyebrows. "Oh, really?"

Good grief.

She set her mug on the coffee table and stood. "I can't afford to forget about everything else. I have a daughter who needs me, a business to run. I need to stay focused."

"What about me, Josie?" Nick slowly moved to his feet and faced her. He placed his hands on her shoulders. "I get complicated. But I need you, too."

She gripped his forearms. "For how long?" Until someone with fewer problems comes along?"

A muscle jumped as he clenched his teeth together. He stared at her. "Are you serious? You really think you're just a diversion?" He took her hand and placed it against his chest. "Josie, there is no one better. You...you fill this huge space that's been vacant in me for so long. You and Hannah—you two complete me."

She wanted to believe him. Really, she did.

Nick stared at the split-level ranch with its gray siding, blue shutters and white trim owned by his soon-to-be father-in-law. Or so he hoped.

Nothing to be afraid of. Except the latter. The core of his anxiety.

But he had promised Josie he wasn't going anywhere. What better way to prove he was in it for the long haul than to propose? She'd say yes and then he'd have the family he craved.

Before he asked Josie, he needed to settle things with her father. Call him old-fashioned, but before he proposed, he needed Mr. Peretti's blessing.

If the man didn't slam the door in his face first.

He straightened his collar, brushed invisible lint off his jacket and rang the doorbell.

When the door opened, Mr. Peretti's frame filled the threshold. "Nick, come in."

Nick held out his hand. "Thank you, sir. I appreciate you meeting with me."

Mr. Peretti shook Nick's hand. "You said it was important." He stepped aside and let Nick pass.

Noticing Mr. Peretti's sock-covered feet, Nick slipped off his loafers and toed them on the mat near the door. The house smelled like freshly baked cookies and lemon furniture polish.

"Have a seat in the living room." Mr. Peretti nodded to the room to the left of the door. "Gracie made coffee and just pulled a fresh batch of cookies from the oven. I'll be right back."

Nick moved into the living room. White upholstered furniture outlined a large Oriental rug patterned in blues and greens covering the gleaming hardwood floor. Framed photos hung on light green walls. White curtains hung from the ceiling-to-floor windows, allowing natural light to warm the room. A brightly lit aquarium filled with colorful fish gurgled in the corner of the room near one of the windows.

He picked up a photo in a silver frame that showed Mr. Peretti in a dark suit standing next to Mrs. Peretti wearing a lace gown and holding a bouquet of flowers. Their wedding picture.

Mr. Peretti returned carrying a tray. He handed Nick a thick ceramic mug full of steaming coffee. Nick sipped it. Not bad. Nothing like Josie's coffee, but drinkable.

Grabbing his own cup, Mr. Peretti sat and leaned back, resting his ankle on his knee. He gestured for Nick to sit. "So, what's on your mind?"

The older man's relaxed demeanor didn't deceive Nick. He set his cup on the floor, away from his feet so he wouldn't knock it over. That would go far in making a good impression. "Sir, we didn't meet during the best of circumstances. I'm sorry for that. I've missed out on so much of Hannah's life. If I could turn back time.... Well, anyway, regrets won't get me anywhere."

"The past is in the past." Mr. Peretti reached for the plate of cookies and handed it to Nick. "Focus on the present and don't make the same mistakes in the future."

Nick took a cookie. Instead of eating it, he rotated it in his fingers. "I'm trying not to. I mean I don't plan to." Why did he have to babble like an idiot?

Setting the cookie on his knee, Nick tugged on his collar. He had been less nervous when he'd had to defend his doctoral thesis. Sweat trickled between his shoulder blades. "I'm still trying to wrap my head around the idea of fatherhood, but I couldn't ask for a greater gift. Hannah's amazing."

"She's a lot like her mother."

"Yes, she is. The thought of going back to work and seeing her only a couple of times a week isn't something I really want to think about."

"So, what are you going to do?" Mr. Peretti took a sip of his coffee, his eyes not leaving Nick.

"Well, that depends on Josie."

"In what way?"

"Before I answer that, sir, there are a few things you need to know about me. About my past." Telling Josie about what had happened that night had been tough. But facing her father—man, he needed strength greater than his own to get through it. Nick exhaled and shared the same sordid story with Josie's father and prayed the man didn't kick him to the curb.

"That's everything." Nick stopped talking and focused on the fish swimming in the aquarium. His gut churned. A mantel clock ticked in the quiet room.

"Son, you've had it rough. I'll give you that. When I

married Josie's mother, she wasn't a Christian. I was so in love with that girl and thought I could change her. I was wrong. Being married and having a family wasn't a part of her life plan. She left us to go find herself. I don't want Josie facing the same thing. So I have to ask—where does God play into your life?"

"I gave my life to God back in college. Since the accident, though, I doubt He wants much to do with me. I'm not going to be listed in the Christian Hall of Fame or anything."

"Only One is good enough for that honor. Thanks to God's grace, we can be used by Him for His purpose. Don't let evil pollute your thinking—God still loves you, no matter what. Keep trusting in Him. A few minutes ago, I asked what you were going to do about Josie."

Nick closed his eyes, scrubbed a hand over his face then faced Mr. Peretti. "Even though I haven't been back in Josie's life very long, I can't imagine my life without her now. I love her, sir. And I'd like your permission to marry your daughter."

Chapter Sixteen

Only a fool would let a man break her heart twice. And Josie Peretti was no fool, despite her recent heart revelation.

Watching Nick help Hannah untangle the kite string—the patient way his large fingers worked at the tiny knots—crumbled the last brick around her heart. Apparently he was successful because Hannah started clapping and jumping up and down, her hat flopping against her forehead. Nick picked her up with one arm and pulled her to his chest. Hannah wrapped her arms around his neck.

When Nick left, Josie's heart wasn't going to be the only one to break.

She had to protect her daughter. Isn't that what good mothers did?

If only she could believe he was really in it for the long haul.

Josie stretched out, leaning back on her elbows. She drew in a deep breath, filling her lungs with the crisp April air soaked with the promise of spring. Fingers of sunshine caressed her face. In front of her, the lake lapped at the shoreline. The breeze rippled the surface of the bluish-gray water. In the budding branches above her, birds tweeted to their neighbors.

What a rare treasure today turned out to be. In more ways than just the weather.

She had finished the lunch rush—*Thank You, God, for answered prayers about business picking up*—when Nick and Hannah came into the shop, carrying a wicker picnic basket and a multicolored butterfly kite.

Hannah's gentle pleading had Josie doing something she hadn't done since she opened the shop—she played hooky. The joy on her daughter's face shoved away any traces of guilt.

Josie dug through her tote bag for her digital camera. She set it to video, zoomed in on father and daughter and recorded their first attempt at getting the kite in the air.

Nick held on to the kite as he walked backward on the sand in bare feet and jeans rolled above his ankles. His untucked white button-down shirt billowed in the wind.

Josie shifted the camera to Hannah, who kept one hand pressed to the top of her floppy denim bucket hat and gripped the spool of kite string with the other. With the weather in the low 50s, Josie hoped her daughter was warm enough in her cropped denim jacket, teal T-shirt and white leggings. Her cheeks had a tinge of color.

Nick released the kite. It buoyed in the air and then hitched a ride on a wind current, gliding higher into the sky. Nick jogged across the sand and knelt behind Hannah, showing her how to let out just enough string to let the kite dance.

The butterfly with its purple, green and bright pink wings dipped and soared, its turquoise tails trailing behind.

Hannah giggled.

Josie zoomed in as Nick pressed a kiss on Hannah's cheek. He looked over at Josie and waved at her to join them. Still filming, she walked slow and steady until she reached the lip where grass and sand met.

Lakeside Family

Nick strode over to her. "Why don't you take a turn with her and I'll man the camera?"

"Thanks."

Josie hurried to Hannah and wrapped an arm around her daughter's shoulders. "You doing okay, babe?"

"Yes, this is fun. Thanks for coming, Mom. Want a turn?"

"Sure." Josie accepted the plastic reel, surprised by the pull of the kite still soaring above the trees. Hannah's joy buoyed Josie's heart as the two of them guided the kite higher. A few minutes later, she handed the reel back to Hannah. "Can you handle this on your own for a couple of minutes? I need to talk to Nick."

"I'm not a baby."

Josie dropped a kiss on her daughter's forehead. "You'll always be my baby. Shout if you need a hand."

Josie returned to the blanket where Nick sat with his knees pulled up and elbows propped. The camera lay on the red plaid blanket. Josie sat next to him and scrubbed her feet in the cool grass to get rid of the sand before she pulled her socks back on.

Still focused on Hannah, Nick nudged her with his shoulder, causing her to topple sideways. "Remember the Ridgefield Kite Festivals?"

"They were a blast, especially when your dragon kite took off! Mr. Malone's toupee."

"He was a good sport about it. After that, he left the tacky thing at home and proclaimed bald was beautiful." He grinned, his eyes hidden behind his aviator sunglasses.

A pod of butterflies did their own soaring in the pit of her belly. She reached for her other sock just as Nick slid an arm around her and gave her shoulder a gentle squeeze. Her hands stilled. She stared at the white cotton in her hand. Two more inches and she could rest her head on his shoulder.

Was that what she wanted?

Oh, yes.

She turned to find Nick staring at her. This time, his sunglasses were off. She could see her reflection in his chocolate-brown eyes.

And she wanted him to kiss her in the worst way.

As if reading her mind, Nick slid his hand around the back of her head, twining his fingers in her short layers. His thumb brushed the sensitive area behind her ear. She shivered. His warm breath caressed her cheek as Nick lowered his head and claimed her lips as his own.

He smelled of fresh air, springtime promises and hope. The sensation of his lips over hers, the awareness of his closeness dogged her. Love didn't stick around. She knew that. But if only she could convince her head and her heart to come to some sort of an agreement. Otherwise they'd have to go into mediation, and she didn't even want to consider that outcome.

"Are you two going to get married?"

Nick and Josie jerked apart. Hannah stood in front of them, her twiglike arms crossed in front of her, one foot tapping like a disapproving parent. Except instead of a scowl, a grin creased her heart-shaped face.

Chuckling, Nick scrubbed a hand over his face, but not before Josie caught the red darkening his neck.

Nothing like a kid to put them on the spot.

Josie shoved her feet into her shoes and stood, brushing the seat of her pants. Over the top of Hannah's head, she saw the kite lying on the beach. "What happened to the kite?"

"I got bored standing there by myself."

"I'm sorry, babe."

"So, did you and Dad have a lot to talk about?"

Josie felt heat climb her own neck. Instead of answering Hannah's question, she asked, "Hungry? Ready for lunch?"

"Can I make a sand castle first?"

"As long as you promise to stay out of the water."

"I promise." Hannah grabbed her pink bucket and net bag full of sand toys. "Dad, wanna help me?"

"Okay." Hannah returned to the sand and dumped out a shovel, bucket and plastic shapes.

Josie knelt on the blanket and opened the picnic basket. The back of her neck prickled. Without looking over her shoulder, she knew Nick was watching her. Hopefully if she pretended like nothing happened, he'd forgot about their kiss and their daughter's insane question.

Marriage. Right.

Like Nick would want to marry her.

But what if he did?

What would she say?

She gave her heart to him once, only to have it returned in pieces. Would he handle it with care this time?

"Josie." Nick whispered her name as he touched her elbow.

Eyes fixed on the egg salad sandwiches and carrot sticks inside the basket, Josie sat back on her heels and wiped her hands on her jeans. "Nick."

"Look at me."

She did as instructed. The tenderness in his eyes and the slight upward tug of his lips nearly had her launching herself back in his arms.

"Hannah." Josie gestured toward the sand. "She's just... she doesn't understand."

Nick leaned back, stretching his long legs out in front

of him. "Actually, I think she understands perfectly." He shifted and reached for Josie's hands.

She had no choice but to sit and face him. Otherwise, she'd be off balance and end up in his lap. Facing him was much safer.

"We can tiptoe around the elephant or we can deal with it."

He was right, but she was a little afraid of Nick's response.

"Josie, from the moment I met you back in high school, I knew you were something special. The girl I once knew has been replaced by a woman whose heart and generosity are larger than anything I've ever experienced. You're a terrific mother who will do anything for her daughter, including letting a guy like me into your lives. These past weeks have shown me how important family really is. I want a real family, but I want it with you and Hannah. I can help you out with the shop and be there for Hannah." Nick pulled a small black box from his front pocket, flipped it open and presented it to her. "Josephina Elenora Peretti, will you marry me?"

Afternoon sun reflected off the princess-cut solitaire flanked by two smaller diamonds on a platinum band and sent a prism of color across the ivory satin.

Josie's breath caught in her windpipe. She pressed a palm to her chest. She looked at him, waiting to see if he had anything else to say.

Just say them—three little words.

After a minute of him watching her with that hopeful expression on his face, she guessed he was waiting for an answer without adding anything else.

What about love?

He hadn't said he loved her. She loved him. But she wouldn't commit to a man who couldn't love her back.

She'd rather spend the rest of her life as a single mother than end up divorced like her dad.

Nick talked about helping her with the shop and being there for Hannah, but what about her? How did he feel about her? She wanted him to love her. Not just for Hannah or for old time's sake, but the new and improved Josie.

This wasn't about her at all. This was about him needing to save everyone, fixing their problems.

He was so sure she would have said yes. Otherwise, he wouldn't have blurted out the proposal like that. What did he say that had her snagging Hannah and darting to her car like a rabbit being pursued by a fox?

He should have kept his big mouth shut. Then he wouldn't be sitting on the end of the dock with his daughter's barrage of questions echoing in his ears because her mother was too much of a coward to face what she was really feeling.

She didn't say no.

In fact, Josie said nothing.

She helped Hannah shove her toys in the bucket and left, leaving behind the kite and the lunch he had packed. Hannah's bewildered expression was imprinted in his head. Now he looked like a jerk to his daughter, too. What had Josie told her? Probably not the truth.

Or maybe she did. That would cause a rift between father and daughter. Was that Josie's plan all along—once she didn't need him for the transplant, get his daughter to turn her back on him, too? Josie wasn't like that.

She was scared. He saw it in the deer in the headlights look she gave him.

Nick gripped the edge of the dock, not caring about the splinters that speared his fingers. Pain clawed his chest, begging to be released.

The wind picked up, ruffling his hair. Clouds bullied away the sunshine. The bluish-gray water lapping at the buoys separating the beach from the boating area slid into a metallic silver-black. Gulls screeched overhead.

Across the lake, spindly pines shouldered skeletal trunks. Their budding limbs stretched out spiny talons, beckoning in the gusts that scalloped the water's surface.

Nick felt like a kite that had been dropped in a down wind. He pulled out the velvet box and tossed it back and forth in his hands. He had spent an hour looking at rings until he'd found the one, knowing it would look perfect on Josie's finger. If she said yes.

Which she hadn't.

But a tiny strain of hope tugged on a corner of his heart—she didn't say no, either.

Pushing to his feet, he trudged across the dock. A gust of wind sent Hannah's kite careening across the sand. Raindrops bulleted the water.

He picked up his pace. The kite and basket were going to get wet.

Destroyed.

Like his hope of a family with Josie and Hannah.

Nick jogged through the rain and snatched the kite before it could trip across the sand again.

One of the butterfly wings separated from the support. The tail ripped. The kite could be repaired, but it would be scarred. Like his heart.

Did God even care?

Shoving the kite under his arm, he gathered the blanket, the soaking wet remains of the picnic, and dropped the mess in his truck's trunk.

Chapter Seventeen

❧

Josie wanted a clone—someone who could do her job as well as she did so she could stay in bed with the covers pulled up to her chin while she watched mind-numbing reality TV for at least a week.

She added more flour to the board and kneaded the smooth, warm dough until her muscles ached. The scent of yeast took her back to when she was Hannah's age and watching *Nonna* make bread when *Nonno* managed to annoy her. Some weeks *Nonna* made a lot of bread. But she and *Nonno* always made up with a kiss.

She wiped her cheek on her shoulder, erasing the memory, and glanced at her bare left hand.

Nick had a ring.

And apparently planned the whole crazy proposal thing. Maybe even set Hannah up to ask if they were going to get married. What had he been thinking?

Every time she closed her eyes, the look on Nick's face when she didn't give him an answer to his proposal swam into view.

She grabbed the greased loaf pans and smacked them on the counter next to her bread board, disturbing a puff of flour.

"Mercy, somebody's got her fireballs all lit up with no place to throw 'em." Agnes carried an airpot into the kitchen and set it next to the coffee makers.

"Don't start with me." Josie cut the dough, shaped it into loaves and dropped them in the pans.

"Hey, I ain't lookin' to lock horns with you." Agnes streamed dark roast into one of the airpots, unleashing its rich scent.

Josie breathed deeply, filling her lungs. Every pore in her body begged for the indulgence. Oh, how she craved to pour a cup, wrap her hands around the mug, savor its warmth and sip. But then she'd spend the rest of the day in bed with a migraine to keep her company and a bucket nearby. Needing to care for Hannah trumped her own desires.

Agnes carried the full pot back to the dining room. After one final deep breath, Josie covered the bread pans with a towel and washed her hands.

She scrubbed the flour and bits of dough off the counter and sanitized it, then picked up a piece of paper to see what was next on her baking to-do list.

Agnes poked her head into the kitchen. "So how much longer you going to hole up in here?"

"I have work to do." Josie filled the sink with hot, sudsy water.

"You've been stomping around back here like someone stole your best biscuit recipe. And you haven't set foot in that dining room since you snuck in the back door this morning."

Josie whirled around, bubbles clinging to her hands.

"Are you complaining about being worked too hard, Agnes?"

"This isn't about me, Sugar Pie, so don't get your knickers in a twist." Agnes flounced through the door, giving Josie that "I'm not leaving until you tell me" look. "What's going on with you?"

Josie exhaled, gripped the edge of the sink, locking her elbows. "Yesterday…Nick proposed."

"Well, ain't that a kicker. And that just sticks in your craw?"

"He doesn't love me. He talked about being there for Hannah, helping me with the shop, blah, blah, blah…but he didn't say anything about loving me." Josie caught her reflection in the curve of the faucet. Her frown appeared to be half a mile long. And that was how she felt. Distorted.

"Sugar Pie, that cowboy's been tryin' to tie his horse to your hitching post since he came to town." Agnes pushed away from the counter and moved to the sink. She tucked a loose curl behind Josie's ear. "He's been showing it every day since he rode into town. You're not listening with your heart."

Josie's stomach twisted, remembering the way Nick had reorganized her kitchen while the storeroom was being repaired. She remembered his gentle way of consoling Hannah after she overheard their argument. The way he kissed her. But it wasn't enough. "I want the words, Aggie. Is that too much to ask? I want to be swept off my feet. And I won't settle—even if it means staying single for the rest of my life."

Lime-green and bright pink balloons bobbed against the ceiling, their curling ribbon tails swaying with Justin Beiber's crooning from Josie's docked iPod.

Hannah and four of her friends huddled on the living room floor around an *American Girl* magazine. Glancing up and spotting Josie watching them, Hannah widened her eyes and jerked her head toward the kitchen.

Okay, so maybe she was hovering. Just a little.

Swallowing a sigh, Josie headed for the kitchen as the oven timer dinged. She gloved her hands and lifted homemade pizzas out of the oven, setting the round baking stones on wicker mats. Bubbles of cheese puffed across the top, then popped.

She cut both pizzas and carried them to the dining room table. Her grandmother's crocheted tablecloth had been replaced with a lime-green plastic cloth printed with hot-pink hibiscus flowers. Raffia skirted the table.

Grace ladled tropical punch into plastic coconut-shaped cups. Her dad inserted colorful colored straws and fruit kebabs speared with colorful paper umbrellas before setting them on the table. Lindsey held leis Hannah and Josie had made for each of the girls.

Josie fisted her gloved hands on her hips and surveyed the table. "We're missing something." She wanted this to be the perfect party for Hannah. Her daughter deserved it. And she prayed it wouldn't be her last. She wasn't going there today.

Grace filled the last cup and handed it to Josie's dad. "The girls?"

Josie smiled. "Can't have a party without them." She walked to the doorway and called into the living room. "Okay, girls, pizza's ready."

Her dad plopped a ratty straw hat on his head, spread his arms out wide and greeted the girls in his best island native voice, "Welcome to the island, mon."

Josie nudged him. "Wrong island, Dad."

The girls covered their mouths and giggled as Lindsey placed the leis around their necks. An inflatable coconut tree swayed in an imaginary breeze as the girls skipped past and found their seats. They chattered like myna birds, oohing and aahing over the decorations.

Josie retrieved the docked iPod, plugged it in behind the

buffet, then scrolled to the island music she and Hannah picked out. Strumming ukuleles and gourd drums played in the background.

Grace and Lindsey moved their hands and hips in time to the music. Their impromptu hula generated applause from their audience.

Even though the thermometer hadn't budged past fifty, all three women dressed alike in tank tops and floral-printed sarongs tied at their hips. Josie had worn a long-sleeved, button-down white shirt over her pink tank top and knotted it at the waist. She dug around in her closet for last summer's flip-flops and glued on some of the leftover silk flowers she and Hannah had used to make the leis.

Josie caught Hannah's attention and winked. Hannah's smile reinforced Josie's decision about letting her have the party. Her daughter was happy. That was the important thing. The girls turned their attention more to each other and the pizza than the goofy grown-ups.

Her dad whispered something in Grace's ear. Pink tinted her cheeks, and she gave him a playful smack on the chest. He waggled his eyebrows in response.

Josie turned away. Not because their playfulness embarrassed her, but because she was afraid of releasing the sigh whispering in her heart. She returned to the kitchen. Lindsey leaned against the counter, munching on a cookie. "Okay, so you definitely win the Mom of the Year award. Very cool party, Josie."

"Thanks, I just want Hannah to have a great time. She's been looking forward to this all week." Josie nudged Lindsey aside and reached for the covered circular cake carrier. She removed the lid and inserted ten lime-green candles into a hot-pink frosted flip-flop-shaped birthday cake.

"You have yummy food, cool tunes—for them, anyway—

and lots of activities planned." Lindsey peered over Josie's shoulder. "And with that cake, you're definitely Cool Mom."

"Hannah and I are ready for some sunshine. A luau-themed party was the way to go for us." She swiped a stray blob of frosting off the tray and stuck it in her mouth, her taste buds dancing as the sweetness melted on her tongue. "Warn me if I'm hovering too much."

"This is good for Hannah. And for you, too."

"She was a mess a couple of weeks ago when she didn't go to Ashley's birthday party. That's when I told her she could have one of her own. And then I've been a freak about germs. What if one of them has a cold or something?"

Lindsey gripped Josie's shoulders. "Relax. It's going to work out."

"You're right. I'm worrying for nothing." Josie set the cake on the island and craned her neck to see if the girls needed anything. Grace refilled punch cups and served more pizza. Josie noticed Hannah had barely touched hers. No cause for alarm. Yet. "Hey, are you still okay with giving the girls pedicures later? The nail polish smell won't make you sick?"

"I'll be fine." Lindsey pulled the clear wrap off the dessert plates, grabbed plastic forks and set both on the wicker serving tray next to the cake. "I'm surprised you let Hannah get her ears pierced."

"If you think I'm bad now, you should've seen me at the mall. I asked the girl about a hundred times if her gun was sterile. And Hannah didn't even flinch." Josie dug through the drawer for her cake server and grabbed an ice cream scoop.

"Considering the pokes and pricks she's had in the last six months, I'm not surprised."

"I splurged on the diamonds. Every girl deserves diamonds, especially one who's gone through what Hannah has."

"The wig looks adorable on her."

"I owe Natalie big time for that. Her wig-maker friend worked double duty to get it done on time. They sewed in a soft liner so it's not as itchy. Hannah feels a lot more confident now, especially around her friends."

As if to punctuate that statement, Hannah's giggles wafted into the kitchen, sweetening Josie's heart like cake frosting. She blinked several times to hold back the moisture building behind her eyes.

Lindsey looped an arm around Josie's shoulders and gave her a side hug. "You're a great mom."

She rested her head on her stepsister's shoulder. "So are you. Hope Ty wasn't disappointed he couldn't come to the party."

"Are you kidding? He still thinks girls have cooties. I hope he stays that way for a long time. He's fine with waiting until Sunday when we have the family get-together. You don't think two parties will be too much for Hannah?"

"I'll just make sure she takes it easy tomorrow."

Grace carried the empty pizza stone into the kitchen and set it on the stove. "Ready for round two. I had forgotten how much food a houseful of girls could go through. I remember Lindsey's sleepovers."

"Thanks for helping out tonight, you two."

"I'd do anything for my girls. You know that." Grace hugged Josie, which brought tears to her eyes. Marrying Grace was the best decision her father had made. Grace went out of her way to include Josie and Hannah in her family. And Josie loved having a sister for the first time in her life.

Someone rapped on the back door. Josie looked over

Grace's shoulder as Nick poked his head inside the door. "Can I come in?"

"Nick. Hi." Josie's heart ricocheted against her rib cage. She hadn't really seen him since the disastrous proposal last weekend. He'd tutored Hannah at her house, but had left as soon as Josie came home. Their conversations had been limited to overly polite comments regarding their daughter and nothing more. She missed him.

Nick stepped inside the kitchen, carrying a large square package wrapped in funky flowered paper and crowned with a loopy purple bow. "I probably should've waited until Sunday, but figured I'd drop this off today in case Hannah wanted it early."

Josie pointed toward the living room. "Have a seat in the living room. The girls are just about done eating. Hannah can open her presents in a couple of minutes."

"If you're sure."

No, she wasn't sure. Every time Nick was around, his smile chipped away at the wall around her heart. Seeing him with Hannah made her yearn for what would never be. And now she felt as awkward as a seventh grader talking to the cute boy at the school dance.

She nodded.

Nick slipped off his loafers and strode through the kitchen into the living room.

As soon as he was out of sight, Josie released a breath. "Could that have been any more awkward?"

Grace squeezed her shoulder. "Give it time, honey. Things will be back to normal soon."

"I'm not even sure what normal is anymore. Nick and I haven't been normal since the moment he set foot in the shop." Sighing, Josie herded the girls from the dining room into the living room. She grabbed her camera off the stairs landing and waved for Grace and Lindsey and her father to join them in the living room. Just in time to hear Hannah squeal.

Surrounded by colorful gift bags, Hannah sat Indian-style on the carpet with torn wrapping paper and a box lid by her side. She held something rectangular with a pink cover. "Mom, Dad bought me an iPad! Isn't that, like, the coolest thing ever? I can listen to music, watch movies and even read books on it. And I won't be so bored in the hospital."

"Sweetie, that's fantastic." She hoped she mustered enough enthusiasm.

"And look what else? He found the bunny from *The Velveteen Rabbit*. And I have Birthday Celebration lotion and lip balm." Hannah held up each item, then dropped them back in the box at her feet. She jumped up to hug Nick. "Thanks, Dad. You're the best."

Lindsey leaned over and whispered in Josie's ear. "I thought you were going to buy Hannah an e-reader."

"I did." She thought of the rectangular box hiding in her desk drawer at work.

"I'm sorry." Lindsey squeezed her shoulder.

"I can return it and get her something else." She wouldn't think about the hours she spent searching for Hannah's favorite authors and preloading the books. She'd try to find time tomorrow to come up with something else for Hannah.

"Mom, smell." Hannah stuck a bottle of lotion under Josie's nose. "It really does smell like cake and ice cream."

"Isn't he so thoughtful." Josie smiled, but inside she wrestled with the flaming tail of the green-eyed monster uncurling in her stomach. Parenting wasn't a competition, but why did Nick get to come in and be Cool Dad? She'd practically begged Nick not to buy expensive gifts for Hannah. And, of course, he didn't listen. Nick did exactly what he wanted.

Nick frowned at Josie's words, but she looked away. "Excuse me. I need to check something in the kitchen."

Josie pulled ice cream from the freezer and set in on the counter to soften. She wiped her cold hand on her hip.

"Josie." Nick's hand settled on her shoulder. She jumped. "You okay?"

She moved away from his touch. "Of course. Just getting cake and ice cream ready."

"You seem upset."

"I'm fine." She smiled, but her facial muscles stiffened.

"Are you mad at the gift I bought Hannah? I know it's a little expensive, but it's my first birthday of hers to celebrate. I wanted it to be special."

"The gift is great. She loves it, Nick." Of course she did. Who wouldn't love such an expensive gift for her tenth birthday? It was all she could do to scrape together enough cash for this party and the e-reader. The rest of the month was going to be tight, but Josie didn't care—Hannah was going to be ten only once.

"Then what is it?" He fingered the flower she had pinned in her hair above her ear.

Josie moved away from him to dig through the drawer for the ice cream scoop. Then she remembered it was sitting on the island next to the cake and ice cream. "I found an e-reader on sale and bought it for her."

Nick leaned against the counter and rubbed his eyes with his thumb and forefinger. "I'm sorry. I should've talked to you first. I can take it back."

"Seriously? Are you kidding me? She loves it. I'll return mine for something else." And buy a grown-up attitude while she was in the store. It was silly to be upset with

Nick, but Josie had been the only parent Hannah had known, and now she had to share.

"Listen, can we talk? I mean, later after things settle down a bit." Nick cupped her elbow, his thumb caressing her skin. "I handled things badly last week. Give me a chance to apologize. Let me take you to dinner."

"Nick, I don't know——"

Lindsey burst into the kitchen, her face pale. "Josie, come quick, something's wrong with Hannah!"

Josie rushed to the living room to find her daughter's lips had swollen twice their size. Hives broke out on her face, hands and arms. Her breathing came out in high-pitched wheezes.

Josie dropped to her knees and cradled Hannah. "Nick, call 911. She's having an allergic reaction. Lindsey, grab her EpiPen off the island in the kitchen. Hurry!"

Within seconds, Lindsey thrust the pen in Josie's hand. Josie flicked off the safety release cap and thrust the pen into Hannah's thigh until it clicked. Under her breath, she counted to ten in Italian, each second precious to her daughter's life.

Hannah's breathing lost its high-pitched whistle. Her chest rose and sunk with each labored breath. The blue left her lips, leaving them a pasty gray.

She glanced at the girls. Their eyes widened as they huddled together on the couch. "What happened? Did anyone see?" She should've been in here, watching her daughter. Instead, she did an emotional dance with Nick in the kitchen. Not anymore.

Hannah's friend Ashley glanced at her friends. "She was fine, Ms. Peretti. We put her new lotion on our hands. Hannah put lip balm on her lips. After that she started talking funny and her lips swelled up."

Josie scanned the carpet. "Where's the lip balm?" Where was that ambulance?

"It's still in her hand."

Josie pried Hannah's fingers open and picked up the lip balm, reading the label. Birthday cake scent with vanilla and shea butter.

Her blood turned to ice. The shea butter. And the lotion probably had the same ingredient. She snatched the bottle still open in the middle of the floor and read the label. Yep, same stuff. And Hannah had used enough to cause an allergic reaction. Josie's heart plummeted. She should've been in here.

Sirens wailed outside. About time.

Two EMTs in blue pants and jackets carried large first aid boxes and pulled a gurney. One of the men cupped an oxygen mask over Hannah's nose. Working quickly, they placed her on the gurney and rolled her outside to the ambulance. Josie jogged alongside, the chilly air biting at her bare legs. But she didn't care. She wasn't letting Hannah out of her sight again.

Once they lifted her inside, the one who administered oxygen—his uniform identified him as Hurst—motioned for Josie to climb inside. "You can sit there." He pointed to a bench along the wall of the ambulance.

Josie reached for Hannah's hand and sat. The smell of antiseptic permeated the air. She tried to listen to what the EMTs were saying, but Hannah's shallow breathing and translucent skin tone held her attention hostage.

Hannah flinched when the EMT inserted an IV into her left hand. Josie stroked her forehead. The wig dislodged, revealing her downy-covered head. She straightened the wig.

She jostled in her seat as the ambulance crossed the railroad tracks, then turned onto Hospital Drive and backed into Shelby Lake Memorial's emergency department. The driver wrenched open the back door, and the two men guided the gurney out. The one with Hurst stitched on his shirt wheeled Hannah down the corridor while the other one shared her vitals and other information with the physician on call.

Unfortunately Josie knew the emergency department well enough to map it in the dark. The physician looked familiar, but his name escaped her. She couldn't worry about that right now, anyway, when Hannah appeared small and fragile on the gurney. She caught some of the EMT's words and had been in and out of the hospital enough times to realize Hannah might not come home this time.

Chapter Eighteen

His mother. Ross. And now Hannah. He had no right to a family. You don't hurt those you love.

Nick sprinted across the parking lot and strode into the emergency department. His eyes swept the room with its rose-colored vinyl chairs that formed a horseshoe around a square glass table littered with worn magazines. An elderly man watched some show on the wall-mounted TV while the woman beside him napped with her head on his bony shoulder. In the corner, a teenager in baggy clothes slouched in a chair and played a handheld game.

Striding to the triage desk, Nick cleared his throat. The nurse wearing blue scrubs and a white sweater looked up from her computer. "May I help you?"

Sweat slicked his skin. Nick brushed a palm over his forehead and forced back the bile searing his throat. "My daughter. She was just brought in by ambulance. Hannah Peretti."

"Right. This way, Mr. Peretti." She hefted her oversize form off the small computer chair and lumbered through the swinging doors that led to the exam rooms.

He didn't take time to correct her about his name.

Instead, his muscles tightened as he followed her down the corridor to the last room on the left.

She waved a hand at the door, as if presenting a four-star hotel room. "Here you go."

"Thanks." Shoving his hands in his pockets, his feet froze in the doorway. His daughter appeared swallowed by the bed. The bright lights and white-as-snow sheets washed out her color even more, leaving her skin a sickly blue-gray tone. Tubes ran into her nose and out of her arms.

For as much time as he'd spent in the hospital with Ross, he should be used to the hospital sounds—the whooshing and beeping of the medical equipment, the hushed murmur of voices, the occasional whimper of pain. But as long as he had a breath in his body, he wouldn't get used to the sounds that signaled life or death.

A fist of regret clamped his heart so tightly that he winced and rubbed the left side of his chest. At that moment, Josie looked up and started at seeing him standing in the doorway. The look that crossed her face caused his insides to wither.

She whispered something to the nurse before stalking to him. Her eyes flashed.

His gut burned. "How's Hannah?"

Grabbing his arm, she jerked him outside of the exam room and into an empty consultation room next to Hannah's. Once inside she snapped on the light and closed the door. She crossed her arms over her chest. "How do you think she is, Nick? My daughter is in there fighting for her life. Because of you."

He ground his teeth and steeled his tone. They were not going through this again. "She's my daughter, too."

"A good father wouldn't give his child something that could possibly kill her."

"I am a good father, Josie, and you know it. This was an

accident. I didn't know it would cause a reaction. You told me about the peanut allergy, but never mentioned anything about shea butter."

"So this is my fault?"

"It's no one's fault. It was a stupid accident."

"One that may cost Hannah her life." Her voice choked. She pressed a fist against her lips.

Nick gathered her to his chest. "Don't cry. The doctors will give her something to stop the reaction."

Josie pushed out of his arms. "She's not like other kids. She won't just bounce back from this. Don't you get it? This could kill her. She's all I've got."

"You have me."

Josie looked at him a moment, then shook her head. "No, Nick, I don't."

Her whispered words carved his heart into pieces. "Don't...don't say that. I've spent the last month trying to show you that we're meant for each other."

Josie dragged a hand through her hair, dislodging the flower tucked behind her ear. It spiraled to the floor. "The last month has been a cakewalk compared to what's to come. Are you ready for that? Are you ready to wake up each morning and pray your daughter wakes up, too?"

"Where's your faith, Josie? You have to believe Hannah will get better. And to answer you, yes, I am ready for all of that. What do you say? Give us a chance." He picked up the flower and twirled it between his fingers.

She held up a hand. "I can't deal with this right now. My daughter needs me."

He sandwiched her hand with his. "She's my daughter, too. And I need you."

"For how long, Nick?" Her eyes searched his face.

His heart plummeted. He dropped her hands and took a step back. "It's never been a matter of if I'd leave you again, but *when*, right, Josie? I'm not that nineteen-year-old kid anymore. And I'm not your mother. I'm here for the long haul, whether you want me to be or not, so you'd better get used to having me around."

His phone rang in his shirt pocket. He glanced at the display. Jacob House. He grabbed it. "Nick Brennan."

"Nick? Walt here. Hey, listen. Ross can't find his camera and is becoming increasingly upset. Don't suppose you have it, by chance, do you?"

An ache pulsed behind his eyes. He didn't have time to worry about a camera right now. "No, I haven't seen it."

"Ross keeps asking for you. Do you have time to stop by?"

Nick's shoulders slumped as he leaned against the wall. How could he be in two places at once? "I'm at the hospital. My daughter had an allergic reaction. I'll check my truck to see if the left it in there and call you back." He ended the call and gripped the phone. "I have to run out to my truck, but I'll be right back."

Reaching for the handle, Josie wrenched the door open. "You know what, Nick? Don't bother. I'll handle this without you." She stormed out of the room.

Nick locked his hands behind his head and pressed his forearms against the sides of his head. He squeezed his eyes shut and fought the impulse to shove his fist through the light box.

He left the room and paused outside Hannah's door. She lay in the bed with her eyes closed. He ached to go inside, to kiss her forehead and tell her how sorry he was, that he didn't mean to screw it up. But sorry wouldn't cut it. Was she better off without him?

He turned and headed down the corridor when his phone rang again. He jerked it out of his pocket. The university. What now?

One of the nurses looked up from the clipboard. "Sir, you can't have cell phones in this department."

Nick nodded and strode toward the red EXIT sign. Instead of exiting into the emergency waiting area, he ended up in an unfamiliar hall. The phone still clenched in his hand continued to ring. He answered just to silence the annoying sound and pushed through the first door he saw.

"Dr. Brennan." His eyes took a few seconds to get used to going from an overly bright corridor to a low-lit room with flickering candles on a side table.

"Dr. Brennan, this is Dr. Clark. Your family leave is up soon, and the department would like to sit down with you before you return to the classroom."

One more person demanding his attention. He heaved a sigh and dropped onto the closest chair. "I'm sorry, Dr. Clark, but I will have to call you back. My daughter is in the hospital."

"The meeting requires your attention."

"What's it about, sir?" He gripped the back of his neck and rolled his shoulders to loosen the tight muscles.

"Due to the recent…information you shared about your daughter, some of the board members are concerned about your name being linked to the university."

"My daughter has no bearing on my role as a professor at the university."

"What about those impressionable kids? What would they think?"

"Those students aren't kids. They're adults who make choices regardless of what gossip they may hear on campus." Nick ground his teeth.

"You still need to lead by example." Dr. Clark's patronizing tone dripped in Nick's ear.

Nick fought to keep his voice level. "My example is I'm manning up to be a responsible father. If that's a sore spot with the university, then I will have my resignation letter on your desk by the end of the week. Good day, Dr. Clark." He ended the call.

What had he done?

He had a family to provide for. He couldn't mouth off to his department chair and quit. Just like that. And he had Ross to think about.

Chest heaving, his blood raced through his veins.

Dropping the phone on the floor, he rested his elbows on his knees and pressed his hands to his face. His daughter was at death's door. Josie hated his guts. His brother needed him. Josie expected him to walk out the door any moment. He was no good to any of them.

Or to God.

He opened his eyes to find a plain wooden cross at the front of the room haloed by an overhead light. A small altar had been placed in front of it.

He had no right being here.

Pushing to his feet, he walked past four rows of padded chairs until he stood in front of the cross. Shadows flickered across the floor. Piped-in music sang of God's amazing grace.

Nick choked back a fist-size lump and squeezed his eyes shut against the surge of wetness. He dropped next to the altar and drove his hands through his hair. He fixed his eyes on the diamond-patterned carpet, counting the shapes between his feet as he forced his breathing under control. His keys dug into his thigh. Stretching out his right leg, he pulled them out of his pocket. The Superman key chain mocked him.

He was nobody's hero.

A hand clamped on his shoulder. He jerked up, dropping his keys. Emmett Browne stood behind him wearing his tweed hat. Compassion lined his face.

Leaning on his cane, Emmett eased himself next to Nick. He nodded over Nick's shoulder. "Didn't mean to eavesdrop, but I was sitting in that first row when I heard you on the phone. Wanna talk about it?"

Nick steepled his trembling fingers and shook his head. "You just happened to be here?"

"Gideon volunteers in the cafeteria. I come in here and think. And pray. Got in the habit when my wife was in the hospital. Now I like the quiet." Emmett cupped the end of his cane, then leaned down to retrieve Nick's keys. He ran a thumb over Superman. "Ross calls you Super Nick."

"The kid doesn't know what he's talking about."

"I think he does."

Nick swiped the keys from Emmett, jumped to his feet and shoved them in his front pocket. "Are you crazy? I'm nobody's hero. M-my daughter is fighting for her life because of me. Josie never wants to see me again. My brother can't remember one day to the next because of me. The kid's freaking out right now because he can't find his camera. And now I have no job. Some hero. I can't even take care of my own family." He scrubbed a hand over his face, disgusted with himself to find his fingers damp.

"For someone with a Ph.D., you can act pretty stupid at times." Emmett studied him a moment. Leaning on his cane, he shuffled to his feet. "How about I tell you what a real hero looks like?"

Nick wanted to stomp out of the room where the dimly lit walls wouldn't feel as if they were closing in on him. He wanted to turn back time. Rewind the past sixty minutes. Or even the past ten years. Defeat weighing heavily on his shoulders, Nick sat in one of the chairs at the front of the room.

Emmett cleared his throat. "I've been watching you. I see the way you are with that pretty little girl of yours. And your brother. Gideon tells me how you visit Ross every day and look at his pictures or do puzzles. When you're around, Josie has a skip in her step."

"That's not heroism."

"Listen, son. I know all about feeling sorry for yourself. Did it plenty of times, especially after my wife died and I rattled around in our big old house by myself. Christopher Reeve said a hero is an ordinary individual who finds the strength to persevere and endure in spite of overwhelming obstacles. He knew a thing or two about being a superhero."

Groaning as he angled his body next to Nick, Emmett stretched out a leg, rubbed his knee and sighed. "I may be the grumpy old codger who snarls about bran muffins and hogs the morning paper, but I know a good guy when I see one. You're the family glue. Ross isn't perfect, and you love him completely. God doesn't expect perfection. He has that gift of grace. You've stepped up. Now you need to accept His grace. In my eyes, that's a hero, son."

Emmett's words washed over Nick, soaking into every pore. Was it true? God didn't expect him to be a superhero? Nick hadn't leaned on anyone in a long time. Usually he was the strong support for others. And right now, he felt about as weak as melted candle wax.

Lord, I'm tired. Tired of not living up to expectations. Tired of feeling like a screw up. I need Your grace and help to put my family back together. Help me to lean on You.

His eyes filled. Bowing his head, he let the tears slide down his cheeks and drip onto the carpet.

Chapter Nineteen

Birthdays were supposed to be days of celebrations, not spent fighting to breathe in a hospital room painted the color of chicken soup.

Children's laughter should be echoing through the room instead of beeping monitors and hissing tubes. The scent of sulphur from extinguished birthday candles should be lingering in the air. Not the stench of disinfectant that had become as familiar as Josie's own shampoo.

Her gaze fixated on Hannah's sleeping form, memorizing every curve and line of her face. As if she hadn't already done that. Her daughter's chest rose and fell in a peaceful rhythm. Too peaceful, too final.

One more birthday, God. Please.

She'd pray that prayer every day for the rest of her life, if she had to.

Josie couldn't bear the pain of going through life without her only child. And losing another person she loved would surely shred her heart beyond repair. But her daughter was more than that. She was a piece of her. A small representation of the good in Josie's life.

She swiped at the tears crowding her eyes, swallowing back the boulder-size lump that seemed to be a constant part of her anatomy. Hope appeared to be the far-off tanker in the middle of the ocean, and she resided on the island of despair with rescue being an oh-so-distant stranger.

And when Nick walked away, he took a piece of her heart with him. Would he return? The voice inside her head screamed for him to stay. She couldn't bear to be alone anymore, to lose someone else she loved. Why had she told him not to bother coming back?

What was wrong with her?

She was raised to treat people better than that. Once he left and reason pushed away her judgment, she realized the allergic reaction truly was an accident. Hannah's pediatrician mentioned that few cases had been documented. With Hannah's latex and nut allergies, though, her body was susceptible to being allergic to the shea nut and proteins used in body care products.

So Josie needed to indulge in a helping of humble pie.

She looked up as Dad walked into Hannah's room with a bag slung over his shoulder, a Cuppa Josie's cup in one hand and in the other, a bouquet of daisies that appeared to have been dipped in a rainbow. Raindrops dotted his jacket.

The explosion of color brightened the generic room with its muted pastel floral border, gleaming tile floors and blue privacy curtain that matched the chair Josie had been sitting in for more hours than she cared to remember.

"Hey, Dad." She rose to hug him and took the flowers from him, setting them on the table next to Hannah's bed.

He dropped the bag on the floor and handed her the cup. "Hi, honey. It's beginning to rain. Here's the stuff you asked for. And some tea. How's our birthday girl?"

"Thanks. She's tired, but stable. They gave her something to help her sleep and want to keep her overnight for observation." Josie handed the cup back to her dad, unzipped the bag and pulled out jeans and a pink sweater. She gestured toward the bathroom. "I'll be right back."

Minutes later, Josie returned and tucked her folded sarong, shirt and tank top in the bag.

"How you doing, sweetheart?" Dad turned away from Hannah and gave her his best principal look.

"Fine." What could she say? Rotten? Ashamed of herself? Terrified out of her mind?

Dad hooked an arm around her neck and pulled her close, kissing the top of her head. "Okay, now tell me the truth."

She wrapped her arms around his waist and leaned her face against the soft fabric of his gray button-down shirt. He smelled of rain-soaked breezes, early morning walks and trust—someone who allowed her to be real without judgment. "Awful."

"Why's that?" He nodded toward the bed. "Other than the obvious, of course."

Returning to her chair next to Hannah's bed, she rested her head against the back and closed her eyes. "Nick and I had a fight. I said some pretty nasty things."

"Stress has a way of making us say things we may regret later." Dad pulled another chair closer to the bed.

Josie winced as it scraped across the floor.

"I don't know if he'll forgive me." She hooked her bare feet over the metal bed railing, wishing she had remembered to ask Dad to grab socks and her shoes. Oh, well, her flip-flops would have to do.

"Don't be so sure." He grabbed the insulated to-go cup off Hannah's bedside table and handed it to her.

She clutched it, breathing in the citrus spice aroma. "Things have been weird between us this past week. Last week he asked me to marry him. Again."

"Again?"

Josie explained about Nick's ridiculous proposal the first night they had been reunited. "And now he asked me to marry him, but it's for Hannah's sake."

"Are you sure it's not more than that?"

"He didn't mention love. Not once."

"Do you love him?"

She sipped her tea, avoiding her dad's eyes. "No...yes."

"Why didn't you tell him that?"

"Seriously? I'm not going to marry someone who doesn't love me. I'm not going have Nick walk out on me when he gets tired of playing family."

Dad leaned forward, resting his elbows on his knees. "Nick is not your mother, sweetheart. He is Hannah's father and needs to shoulder some of the responsibility."

"I've been doing just fine for the past ten years. I don't need his help." She pushed out of the chair and strode to the window. Hannah's room overlooked a lower level of the hospital. Thunder rumbled in the distance. Lightning flashed, reflecting off the silver domes on the roof.

Dad's chair squeaked as he stood and walked to her, placing his hands on her shoulders. "Your pride and willingness to do everything by yourself is a bit selfish, don't you think?"

Josie whirled around, his words wounding her to the core. Nick had said something similar recently. "I'm not selfish."

"But holding these tight reins of not needing anyone else's help is selfish—you're taking the blessing of fatherhood away from Nick. Always having to do things by yourself without asking for help denies someone else the joy or blessing of helping you."

"I just don't want anyone to think I'm not responsible."

"No one thinks that. Where did you get that idea?"

"Gee, Dad, I wonder." Josie waved a hand over her

daughter. "I wasn't the most responsible person ten years ago."

"Are you kidding me? You're the most responsible person I know. Yes, you got pregnant, but you worked hard to provide a life for you and Hannah. At times, you put me to shame."

"I just don't want to end up like Mom."

"You're nothing like your mother, Josie. Where did you get such a crazy idea?"

Josie closed her eyes, hearing the faded anger in her dad's voice as it pierced the walls all those years ago. She had curled up in her comforter and cried herself to sleep. "After I told you I was pregnant, I heard you and *Nonno* talking. You said something about me being irresponsible like my mother."

Dad scrubbed a hand over his face. "I may have spouted off in the heat of the moment, but I never considered you irresponsible, sweetheart. I'm so sorry if I'm the cause of that wound."

She closed her eyes and bathed in the sweetness of being absolved from a lie that weighed her every action. "I just don't want to let anyone down."

"Honey, you're not doing that at all. You're a great daughter, a terrific mother, and your customers love you. Who would you be letting down?"

"I'm sure God's not so thrilled with what I did." Josie grabbed her cup and sipped her tea.

Her dad gave her a compassionate look that patched the wound his words had inflicted a few moments ago. "The Bible is filled with stories of imperfect people being used by God for His glory." He punctuated the air with his hands. "Look at David—he took another man's wife and had her husband killed. Yet, God used him to rule a nation.

And Paul used to persecute the very type of people he later preached to. They had something in common with you."

"What's that?" She sank into the chair by her daughter's bed.

"Grace. God gives us grace. Not because we deserve it, but because of His love for us."

She loved Hannah more than she ever thought physically possible, and there was nothing she couldn't forgive her daughter for doing. So why was it so hard for her to remember that about God? After all, wasn't she His daughter?

Dad crossed to her chair. He touched her head the way she had seen Jesus touch the children in illustrations. A father's love. "You're the one who gets everyone going in the morning. You're quick to offer a smile, a kind word. You have an encourager's heart. So, I think it's time you cut yourself some slack because I think the only person you're letting down is yourself."

"What about Nick?" Josie traced the rim of her cup, allowing his words to soften the rigid expectations she had of herself.

"This isn't my place, but I think it needs to be said so you understand. Princess, that boy is in love with you."

"How do you know?"

"He told me."

Her head jerked up, her heart knocking across her ribs. "He what? When?"

"Last week when he asked for my permission to marry you." A smile tugged the corner of her dad's mouth.

"When he didn't say anything, I just assumed." History was about to repeat itself if she didn't do something about it. Her assumption that Nick wanted to marry her only because of Hannah was going to push him away. Possibly forever this time. She'd been irresponsible in not taking the time to get all the facts before jumping to conclusions. "When Hannah was born and Nick didn't come, I assumed he didn't want us. And now I assumed he didn't want me because he didn't say anything about loving me."

"Have you considered that maybe Nick was scared— afraid for how you felt about him that he didn't want to put himself out there? Nick has suffered loss in his life, too, sweetheart."

"This whole time I've been making it about me." She stood, setting the cup on the table. "I am selfish. I need to find him. But I can't leave Hannah."

"Yes, you can, sweetheart. This is part of that not needing to do everything on your own. I'll stay here with her. I think the two of you could straighten out the majority of your problems by setting aside your pride and having a good old-fashioned conversation."

"I agree."

Josie whirled around to find Nick standing in the doorway, holding Hannah's stuffed alligator, Duck. She wanted to run to him, fling her arms around his neck and beg him to forgive her. But her feet stayed rooted to the tile floor. "Nick. You came back."

"I never left."

Dad nodded toward the door. "You two go talk. I'll stay with Hannah."

Before she could do anything, Nick grabbed her hand and propelled her out of the room and down the hall. He didn't say anything as they moved into the elevator. He jammed the button for the ground floor and kept his eyes fixed on the declining numbers as they lit.

Josie gripped the railing against the elevator wall and tried not to let fear bully her courage. She could do this. She had to. For Hannah. For herself.

The elevator came to a stop. The door dinged, then

opened. Nick stood back to let her exit and joined her in the corridor. "Come with me."

She hurried to keep up with his long strides. He stopped at the door marked Chapel and pushed it open.

The ringing phones, PA announcements and corridor chatter silenced. Josie's eyes adjusted to the change in lighting.

Shadows danced across padded chairs from the flickering votive candles on the side table. The soothing instrumental music coming from a hidden speaker calmed her jittery heart.

They were alone in the room.

Not really.

Josie walked slowly to the front of the room. Her eyes sought the plain cross. She hadn't ever been alone. She sank on one of the chairs. "I've attended church for as long as I could remember. Since Hannah was born, though, I thought I had to shoulder everything by myself. After all, I made my bed."

Nick knelt beside Josie, touching her shoulder. "You've never been alone."

Josie nodded. "I know, but I felt I had to prove myself to be responsible. But I was mistaking responsibility for control. I held on for dear life because if I let go, I was afraid of what God's plan would be for Hannah. I'm tired, Nick. So tired of being the strong one. Tired of putting on a happy face every day. Tired of treading water."

Nick took her hands and pulled her to her feet. "Let go, Josie. I'm here for you. Always."

She launched herself into his arms and closed her eyes as Nick cradled her against his chest. Instead of sinking beneath the surface and drowning, Josie pictured herself being lifted out of life's churning water. She had been rescued.

* * *

Clutching her to his chest, he buried his face in her neck, breathing in the scent of hope and a lifetime of happiness.

"I'm so sorry, Nick. For everything."

"I'm the one who's sorry." His voice choked.

"I said horrible things. I was so scared about Hannah. She's my whole world."

"Is there room in that world for me?"

"I hope so." Josie pulled back and looked at Nick. She rubbed her hand alongside his jaw. "I love you, Nick. When you asked me to marry you—both times—you mentioned Hannah, but nothing about me. I didn't want to be forgotten again. I figured I'd been just fine all this time without you and didn't need you in my life. But this last week has been miserable without you."

"I could never forget you, June bug. I love you." He brushed the pad of his thumb over her cheekbone, wiping away a tear that leaked from the corner of her eye. "I always leave. I'm sorry for the past ten years, but you will never be alone again. I told you I'd never walk out on my family. You are my friend, my love, my family. We will face the future together. This is not the romantic setting I envisioned to sweep you off your feet, but for the third time, marry me?"

Josie eyed him warily. "After all I put you through? Seriously? What kind of woman makes a man ask her three times to marry him before saying yes?"

He slid his fingers through her hair, releasing the floral essence of her shampoo. "The kind I fell in love with, apparently. I'm not so sure I can go for a fourth proposal. So how about an answer?"

"Yes, yes, yes."

"I may be unemployed, by the way."

"Linwood Park is too far away. There are plenty of universities closer to Shelby Lake where you could apply for teaching positions."

"What if I don't teach? I mean, I'll apply for a new position to be able to take care of my family, but I'm considering leaving teaching. How would you feel about that?"

"What are you thinking?"

"I don't know yet. We'll need pray about it, but I've thought about kids like Hannah who may not have parents, money for treatments or support. Maybe we could start a foundation or something called Hannah's Hope. I need to do some research to see what is involved, but I want to reach out to others in need."

"I think it's a beautiful idea."

Josie's cell phone vibrated in her pocket. She fished it out and showed him her father's number on the display.

His gut clenched.

She spoke in low tones, then ended the call. "Dr. Kym is in Hannah's room and would like to talk with us."

Nick stood and pulled Josie to her feet. "No matter what she says, we're in this together."

"Yes. Together." She stood on tiptoe and brushed a kiss across his lips.

Before she could pull away, Nick wrapped his arms around her and kissed her with a soundness that hopefully reminded her how he really felt about her. He couldn't risk losing her again to her own insecurities.

Nick and Josie left the chapel and rode the elevator to the second floor. Hand in hand, they hurried down the hall toward Hannah's room.

Dr. Kym met them outside her door and guided them to a small consultation room. Instead of being dressed in scrubs and a lab coat, Dr. Kym wore a black pencil skirt, white blouse and sensible heels. She gestured to the chairs around the square table.

Once the three of them sat, she opened the folder she'd carried in. "I have Hannah's results. This allergic reaction turned out to be a blessing."

"How so?"

"She has a mild lung infection. Normally it's nothing serious that can't be cured by a round of antibiotics, but Hannah's case isn't typical. I spoke with her team at Mercy Children's Hospital. They want to see her on Thursday. We would like to keep her here, then transport her by ambulance to the children's hospital. That way her antibiotics will be finished before they begin the transplant process." She gave Nick a steady look. "Mr. Brennan, are you still willing to participate as a donor?"

"Absolutely. I'll do anything for my daughter."

"Terrific. I'll notify them right away so we can move forward."

Nick loved the sound of that. Moving forward. A future. With the woman he loved. And his daughter.

He raised Josie's hand to his mouth and brushed a kiss across her knuckles. "We can do this. No matter what happens, I will always be by your side." He'd tell her every hour if that's what it took for his words to sink in.

"No doubt in my mind." The smile she gave him reflected the peace in her eyes.

Josie didn't think her feet touched the floor on the way back to Hannah's room. Her heart felt so light she was afraid it could float out of her chest. Faith and family. What more could a girl want?

She brushed a hand over her forehead. "Hey, sweetie, how do you feel?"

"Hungry." Hannah's voice sounded scratchy.

Josie smiled. "That's a great sign. Anything in particular?"

"Birthday cake?" She gave Josie a sleepy grin.

Dad tweaked Hannah's nose. "I'll let the nurse know."

He gave Josie's shoulder a gentle squeeze.

Nick sat beside Hannah and reached for her hand, careful not to dislodge her IV. "Hannah, I'm so sorry I hurt you."

"It's okay, Daddy. You didn't know." Her eyes struggled to stay open.

"Actually the allergy attack was a good thing. Daddy saved your life." She shared what Dr. Kym had said about the infection and then told Hannah about proceeding with the bone marrow transplant.

Not caring about hospital rules, Josie stretched out beside Hannah. She needed to be close. "Sweetie, there's something else, too."

"What's wrong?"

"Nothing that you don't already know about. Everything's fine." She reached for Nick's hand. "In fact, everything's great."

Nick shuffled to his feet. He wrapped an arm around Josie and one over the top of Hannah's pillow. "Honey, I asked your mom to marry me. I figured it was about time we started being a normal family."

Hannah's eyes darted between the two of them. "And?"

Josie rested her head against Nick. "I said yes."

Hannah's smile spread across her face, rivaling the length of the Shelby River. She shifted to her elbows, struggling to sit up. "Yay! It's about time. When's the wedding?"

Nick pressed a gentle hand against her shoulder, forcing her to rest against her pillow. "We haven't gotten that far yet."

"Mom?" Hannah's gaze shifted to the window. She picked at her nails. "I need you to do something for me."

Josie twined her fingers within Hannah's to stop the anxious action. "Anything."

"When will I have my transplant?"

"You will go to the children's hospital on Thursday." Josie adjusted the blanket around Hannah. "Then they will start you on chemo again and radiation to prepare your body for your dad's stem cells. While that's happening, your dad will have his stem cells harvested. That way, as soon as you're ready, they can transplant them into your body."

"Can you get married before I go?" Hannah scraped her thumbnail across her other nails.

This time, Nick reached for her fingers. "What's the rush, sweetheart?"

"If…if I don't make it…I don't want either of you to be alone. This way, you'll have each other."

Tears flooded Josie's eyes, blurring her vision. Her fingers trembled as she opened the yellow box of hospital-issued tissues. She pulled one out, wiped her eyes and pulled Hannah gently to her. "Sweetie, I will never be alone. Daddy is with me. And I have Jesus. And I promise the doctors will do everything to kick this leukemia. This time next year, you will be laughing and playing with your friends."

"And maybe a baby brother or sister?"

Nick laughed, a hearty sound that bounced off the walls. "Let's not rush it, okay?"

The smile slid from Hannah's face, downturning her lips as she eyed both parents. "Will you do it?"

Josie didn't want to extinguish the wishful light in her daughter's eyes, but she clenched her own hope for Hannah's full recovery. Not that she didn't want to marry

Nick, but she had to trust God to provide a future for her daughter. "Sweetie, let's focus on you getting better. That's what's important right now."

"But you said anything. And this is important. To me. You know...just in case."

Josie turned to Nick and sent him a pleading look. Instead, he grinned at her and tugged on her arm. "Let's talk in the hall. Hannah, we'll be right back."

Nick pulled her across the hall where they could still see into Hannah's room.

"Nick, I'm sorry." Josie pressed her forehead against his chest.

His lips grazed the top of her head. "About what?"

"Hannah. Pushing us to get married."

Nick cupped her face, his eyes growing serious. "Sweetheart, I've spent a lot of time on my knees since the night I saw Hannah for the first time. I'm clinging to hope that God will answer my prayers and give me a lifetime with my daughter. But, she is very sick. If she wants to see us married, then I'm all for it. I wanted to marry you the night I walked into the coffee shop, remember?"

"Yes, and I called you an idiot, remember?"

"I'm your idiot." He grinned.

"Yes, but to get married in less than a week? We've changed so much over the years. I'm not that shy, insecure seventeen-year-old girl anymore."

He cupped her face. "No, you're an amazing woman who juggles her own business, parents the world's most amazing kid and makes a marinara sauce that will make a grown man weep. What more do I need to know? I love you. That will never change."

Josie looked away and traced the knitted weave of his dark green sweater. "I just don't want you to feel rushed. Or regret this later."

He tipped her chin, forcing her to look at him. "I'm not your mother, remember. No regrets."

"We have a crazy road ahead of us. This is not going to be easy."

Lines webbed the corners of his eyes. "June bug, my entire life hasn't been easy. Why should it start now?"

She peered around Nick to see Hannah watching them. With Nick's arms around her, she knew he had the strength needed to weather whatever storms they had to navigate. He proved his worth over and over. Now it was her turn to step out in faith to just trust. She sucked in a deep breath, then exhaled slowly. No turning back. "Okay, then. Let's get married."

Ivory pillar candles of different lengths sat on rectangular mirrors around the hospital chapel and reflected flickering candlelight across the rows of chairs filled with Josie and Nick's family and closest friends. Delicate sounds of Bach's "Jesu, Joy of Man's Desiring" floated over their heads from the hidden sound system.

Grace, Lindsey and Agnes managed to pull a wedding together in three days. Josie couldn't have planned a more perfect wedding if she had spent months preparing. It didn't matter that she was getting married on a Wednesday evening. She hadn't been traditional yet, so why start now? Tomorrow morning Nick would follow the ambulance to Mercy Children's Hospital while she rode with Hannah. They would begin a journey together as they prayed for Hannah's recovery.

But first, she had to get married.

The ceremony had been limited to close family and friends, but a reception for the community followed at Cuppa Josie's. Afterward, Josie and Nick would spend their honeymoon at the Holiday Inn near the hospital.

A shiver of anticipation coursed through her. *Stop it.* She needed to focus.

Dressed in lilac-colored sleeveless dresses, Agnes and Lindsey moved down the aisle. They stopped at the altar and turned to face the guests. Hannah followed behind Agnes, scattering rose petals behind her. Her amethyst-colored dress with its embroidered hem fell below her knees, hiding the thinness of her legs. Her wig had been curled in loose waves that brushed her shoulders.

"Are you sure about this?" Dad, debonair in his black suit, covered Josie's hand tucked in the crook of his arm.

"Absolutely." The best decision she had made so far this year. No, finding Nick topped that. If she hadn't gone to his campus, none of this would be happening now.

The music tempo changed, signaling Josie's turn to walk down the aisle. She touched a hand to her stomach and drew in a shallow breath. The ivory satin of *Nonna's* wedding gown whispered against her skin as she and Dad moved slowly down the aisle.

Her gaze sought out Nick. His eyes darkened as a slow smile spread across his face. Her breathing hitched with expectation.

Beside him, Ross stood as his best man and Emmett leaned on his cane next to Ross, both men looking handsome in their dark suits.

Reaching the altar, Dad lifted her veil long enough to brush a kiss across her jaw. His eyes shimmered as he whispered, "I love you."

She blinked back her own tears. "I love you, too, Dad." Josie handed her bridal bouquet of tulips tied with ivory ribbon to Lindsey and took Nick's hand.

His minty breath warming her neck, he whispered, "You take my breath away."

She gripped his hand and squeezed, not trusting her voice to reply.

Pastor Nate cleared his throat. "Dearly beloved…"

Josie tried to pay attention, but her focus strayed to Nick's thumb caressing her hand. Not to mention he smelled like summer rain and the promise of hope.

Pastor Nate read First Corinthians chapter thirteen as they lit their unity candle together. Then he spoke of everyday love—the kind that is tested daily when the storms of life may come crashing in—and ended by reading the thirteenth verse from Romans fifteen that Josie and Nick had chosen together. *May the God of hope fill you with all joy as you trust in Him.*

Trust hadn't come easily to Josie, but now that she realized her need for control and submitted it to the Lord, joy filled her spirit. Released from the guilt of her past and basking in God's grace, Josie's heart swelled with an intense happiness and an even deeper sense of peace.

With Nick by her side and walking in the love of the Lord, how could they go wrong? Any doubts she may have had disappeared the second she saw him at the front of the church. He was here. Forever.

At Pastor Nate's instruction, Josie and Nick faced each other. As Nick recited his vows, his voice cloaked her soul, blanketing any insecurity with his promises of love. He slid the wedding band they had chosen together onto her finger. A symbol of his love and faithfulness to her.

Her voice wobbled as she promised to love, honor and cherish him until parted by death. A tear slid down her cheek. With his own eyes bright and chin wobbling, he reached over and brushed it away with the back of his hand.

"I now pronounce you husband and wife. Nick, you may kiss your bride."

He closed the distance between them and lifted the

antique lace veil her *nonna* had worn when she pledged her love to *Nonno*. His hands cupped her shoulders as he pulled her closer. His lips brushed hers in a chaste kiss, then claimed her mouth once more. This time his gentleness hinted a deeper desire, a promise of a lifetime of passion. She wrapped her arms around his neck, never wanting to let go.

Nick pulled back, his eyes still bright. "I love you, Mrs. Brennan." His husky voice sent a shiver coursing through her.

She brushed her palm across his cheek. "I love you, too. From the moment I gave you my heart, I knew another man couldn't cherish it the way you do. The way you treasure our daughter and care for your family...you're an honorable man, Nick Brennan. A true hero."

Epilogue

Josie's flip-flops slapped against the wooden planks as she crossed the footbridge over the marsh that led to the private beach. Ocean breezes feathered the leafy palm branches and rustled the sea grasses growing out of the dunes.

Adjusting ten-month-old Noah on her left hip, Josie stopped to kick off her flip-flops and hooked them over her fingers. A seagull landed on the sand next to the beach blanket she had spread out a while ago. Noah squealed, scaring away the bird.

Josie knelt on the blanket and sat her son under the striped umbrella, adjusting his hat and sunglasses. He gave her a drooling toothy grin and pumped his chubby arms. He leaned forward, sprawled on the blanket and grabbed a handful of sand, bringing it to his mouth.

"Oh, Noah, if you eat the sand, then Sissy won't have enough for her sand castle." She dug through the beach bag for the baby wipes and cleaned off his face and hands.

He let out a yelp and twisted in her arms.

Nick strolled over from the sand castle engineering and scooped Noah in his arms. "Hey, buddy, giving your mom a hard time?"

"He wouldn't be a Brennan male if he didn't, would he?"

"Hey, we all have our callings in life." Nick stretched out next to Josie and settled Noah on his chest. "Besides, you wouldn't have it any other way."

Josie handed Noah a plastic sea horse teether, which he shoved in his mouth. "Of course not."

She rolled onto her stomach and rested her chin on her hands to watch Hannah and Ross with their sand castle creation. Her gaze swept the shore and the peaceful waves that lapped at the sand.

The past two years had been some of the toughest of her life, but with God, Nick and prayers from family and friends, they weathered the storms. *Nonna* always said, "God may not calm the storm. Sometimes He calms the child." He became the anchor she needed when they counted down Hannah's days after the transplant—from day zero to day one hundred when she was released from the hospital. With her leukemia in remission, Hannah was making a full recovery.

She peered over her shoulder to find Noah sleeping on his daddy's chest. Nick kept a protective hand on the little guy's back. His other arm supported his head. He nodded toward Hannah and Ross. "So you think she's pleased with her birthday present?"

"You've always given her extravagant gifts." Josie smiled to let him know she was teasing.

Nick raised an eyebrow. "I think this was something we all needed."

"You're so right." Josie shifted to a sitting position and patted Noah's back. "I'm not looking forward to flying home with Mr. Crankypants sleeping on your chest."

"Hey, if you were teething, you wouldn't want to fly, either. At least we have nine more days before we leave. He'll be fine. And you know I've got your back. I've been thinking—perhaps Noah needs a playmate."

"Well, Lindsey and Stephen's next one is due next month." She grinned and touched her stomach. She suspected Nick was going to get his wish sooner than he expected.

He nudged her with his foot. "You're a funny lady, Josephina Brennan."

She released the clip from her hair and let it spill over her shoulders. She grinned and batted her lashes. "How about in seven months?"

Nick sat up quickly, shifting Noah to the cradle in his arm. "Are you serious?"

"I know how much you love being spoiled on Father's Day. Just giving you another reason to celebrate. Of course I'm serious."

Nick's goofy grin dislodged a giggle from her throat. Her heart swelled with joy. She'd come a long way from that panic that had cinched her chest when she'd learned she was pregnant with Hannah. She adored her family, especially since Nick was such a hands-on father. Teaching part-time at a local university and working at Hannah's Hope didn't keep him from spending time with Hannah and Noah.

"As long as they take after you, June bug, I'm totally fine with it." He brushed his lips across hers.

"And if they take after you?"

"Heaven help us all." Nick wrapped an arm around Josie and tugged her back until she sat against his chest. His head rested on top of her head.

She sighed as a breeze blew across her face and danced with her hair. Closing her eyes, she lifted her face to be kissed by the sun's rays.

When Josie learned she wasn't a match for Hannah, she had been forced to find Nick. He turned out to be the miracle she had been praying for, proving God says no for the right reasons. His provision overflowed her heart with joy. By learning to trust in Him, she'd found her happily ever after with the one man she had never wanted to see again. But he was the only one who could cherish her heart and bring them together as a family.

* * * * *

If you enjoyed Lisa Jordan's book, be sure to check out the other books this month from Love Inspired!

Dear Reader,

A mother's worst fear is something happening to her child, whether in the womb or during their developing years. Whether it's a birth defect, cancer or other life-threatening illness, or an accident, her child's life is at risk. The thought of something happening to one of my boys unleashes a coil of fear that grips my heart. Thankfully, neither one of my boys has had a traumatic illness or life-risking accident. But thousands of mothers deal with this on a daily basis.

When I introduced Josie in my first novel, *Lakeside Reunion*, I realized her story needed to be told. Josie struggled with that level of trust—if she released Hannah completely into God's hands, she was fearful about His will for her daughter's life. The thought of losing Hannah numbed her from the inside out. Josie would have done anything to save Hannah, even if it meant reconnecting with Nick. Nick blamed himself for his mother's death and brother's disability. When he learned he had a daughter, and she had leukemia, he vowed to be there for her and Josie. He wouldn't abandon his family. Both Josie and Nick learned God offers us infinite hope. When they trusted in Him, they were filled with joy and peace.

Trust is one of those words that is easy to say, but so much harder to put into action. God cradles each one of us in the palm of His hand. Nothing happens without His knowledge. If you have a child with special needs or one sick with cancer, my heart fills with compassion for you. You may have days of darkness when hope seems like a stranger. I encourage you to put your trust in God and allow His peace to sustain you. You are not alone.

According to the National Marrow Donor Program website (www.marrow.org), 10,000 patients need a marrow transplant, but only half receive one. Please consider joining the Be The Match Registry at www.marrow.org. You could be someone's only hope for a healthy life.

I love to hear from readers! Email me at lisa@lisajordanbooks.com and visit my website, www.lisajordanbooks.com, to learn more about my writing and what's coming up for the residents of Shelby Lake.

Lisa Jordan

Questions for Discussion

1. Josie will do whatever it takes to save Hannah's life, even find the one man who broke her heart. Share a situation where you had to do the last thing you wanted in order to help someone you loved.

2. Josie longs for the day when she and Hannah can build sand castles together on the beach. What glimpse of hope do you have for the future—what is something you'd like to do someday?

3. Nick's father walked out on his family, so Nick vowed never to be like his dad. When he learns he has a daughter, Nick is filled with shame and guilt—he thinks he's like his dad, after all. What past cycle of behavior have you tried to overcome?

4. Josie battles despair—her finances, Hannah's illness, conflicting feelings about Nick—to the point where she's losing her hope. When you feel your circumstances overshadowing your hope, how do you respond? What strengthens your faith?

5. Even though it was an accident, Nick blames himself for killing his mother and causing his brother's disability. What life situation do you blame yourself for? What can you do to let go of that guilt and forgive yourself?

6. Hannah feels like a freak because of her illness and lack of hair. How do you think you would react in her situation?

7. Josie finds comfort in the kitchen—when the going gets tough, Josie gets cooking. What do you do when your security or comfort zone is shaken?

8. Nick's revelation about Hannah puts his job at risk. Share an experience where judgment trumped grace. How did that make you feel?

9. Agnes is a great friend for Josie. She sympathizes, but also points out truth in a loving way. Who is the Agnes in your life?

10. Josie ponders why faith is so easy to have when life is going well, but becomes shaky when life hits a speed bump. When life gets tough, how do you cling to your faith?

11. Nick is the only family Ross has. At times, he becomes overwhelmed by his responsibilities. If you are a parent or caregiver of someone with special needs, how do you handle all of your responsibilities?

12. When Josie learns about Ross from Walt, she feels betrayed and wonders what else Nick is hiding. Then when she learns the truth, she feels compassion and empathy. Describe a time in your life when you jumped to conclusions only to find the truth was different than you imagined.

13. When Nick finally opens up and tells Josie about the accident, it lightens the burden he has carried. Has shame kept your secrets hidden? How did you find freedom from past guilt?

14. Experience taught Josie that love didn't stick around. But then she learned to trust Nick and put her hope in God again. She found her happily ever after. When have you struggled with trusting God? How did you become aware of His presence again and feel His love?

COMING NEXT MONTH from Love Inspired®

AVAILABLE AUGUST 28, 2012

MONTANA DREAMS
The McKaslin Clan
Jillian Hart

Millie Wilson can't blame Hunter McKaslin for his anger upon suddenly learning he's a father—can former sweethearts find a second chance through forgiveness?

CARBON COPY COWBOY
Texas Twins
Arlene James

Though Keira Wolfe doesn't remember much after an accident leaves her in the care of Jack Colby, the rancher proves stronger than her amnesia. the bond drawing her

FINDING HOME
Starfish Bay
Irene Hannon

When Scott Walsh meets widowed mother Cindy Peterson and her sweet boy, he questions his vow never to get involved with a family again.

A MOM'S NEW START
A Town Called Hope
Margaret Daley

Single mother Maggie Sommerfield doesn't know how to help her troubled son—can counselor Cody Weston extend his hurricane recovery efforts to heal this family too?

A DOCTOR'S VOW
Healing Hearts
Lois Richer

After opening a children's clinic, Jaclyn LaForge realizes that her dreams are suddenly coming true—does veterinarian Kent McCloy have a place among them?

CIRCLE OF FAMILY
Mia Ross

When Ridge Collins literally falls out of the sky and into her life, Marianne Weston will need to trust that this pilot has found his greatest adventure yet: family.

Look for these and other Love Inspired books wherever books are sold, including most bookstores, supermarkets, discount stores and drugstores.

LICNM0812

REQUEST YOUR FREE BOOKS!

2 FREE INSPIRATIONAL NOVELS
PLUS 2
FREE
MYSTERY GIFTS

Love Inspired®

YES! Please send me 2 FREE Love Inspired® novels and my 2 FREE mystery gifts (gifts are worth about $10). After receiving them, if I don't wish to receive any more books, I can return the shipping statement marked "cancel." If I don't cancel, I will receive 6 brand-new novels every month and be billed just $4.49 per book in the U.S. or $4.99 per book in Canada. That's a saving of at least 22% off the cover price. It's quite a bargain! Shipping and handling is just 50¢ per book in the U.S. and 75¢ per book in Canada.* I understand that accepting the 2 free books and gifts places me under no obligation to buy anything. I can always return a shipment and cancel at any time. Even if I never buy another book, the two free books and gifts are mine to keep forever. 105/305 IDN FEGR

Name	(PLEASE PRINT)	
Address		Apt. #
City	State/Prov.	Zip/Postal Code

Signature (if under 18, a parent or guardian must sign)

Mail to the **Reader Service:**
IN U.S.A.: P.O. Box 1867, Buffalo, NY 14240-1867
IN CANADA: P.O. Box 609, Fort Erie, Ontario L2A 5X3

Not valid for current subscribers to Love Inspired books.

**Are you a subscriber to Love Inspired books
and want to receive the larger-print edition?
Call 1-800-873-8635 or visit www.ReaderService.com.**

* Terms and prices subject to change without notice. Prices do not include applicable taxes. Sales tax applicable in N.Y. Canadian residents will be charged applicable taxes. Offer not valid in Quebec. This offer is limited to one order per household. All orders subject to credit approval. Credit or debit balances in a customer's account(s) may be offset by any other outstanding balance owed by or to the customer. Please allow 4 to 6 weeks for delivery. Offer available while quantities last.

Your Privacy—The Reader Service is committed to protecting your privacy. Our Privacy Policy is available online at www.ReaderService.com or upon request from the Reader Service.

We make a portion of our mailing list available to reputable third parties that offer products we believe may interest you. If you prefer that we not exchange your name with third parties, or if you wish to clarify or modify your communication preferences, please visit us at www.ReaderService.com/consumerschoice or write to us at Reader Service Preference Service, P.O. Box 9062, Buffalo, NY 14269. Include your complete name and address.

LIREG11B

HARLEQUIN™

SytyCW

SO YOU THINK YOU CAN WRITE

Harlequin and Mills & Boon are joining forces in a global search for new authors.

In September 2012 we're launching our biggest contest yet—with the prize of being published by the world's leader in romance fiction!

Look for more information on our website, **www.soyouthinkyoucanwrite.com**

So you think you can write? Show us!

*When three bachelors arrive on Regina Nash's doorstep,
her entire world is turned upside down.*

*Read on for a sneak peek of HANDPICKED HUSBAND
by Winnie Griggs.*

Available September 2012 from Love Inspired® Historical.

Grandfather was trying to play matchmaker!

Regina's thoughts raced, skittering in several directions at once.

How *could* he? This was a disaster. It was too manipulative even for a schemer like her grandfather.

Didn't he know that if she'd *wanted* a husband, she could have landed one a long time ago? Didn't he trust her to raise her nephew, Jack, properly on her own?

Reggie forced herself to relax her grip on her grandfather's letter, commanded her racing pulse to slow.

She continued reading. A paragraph snagged her attention. Grandfather was *bribing* them to court her! They would each get a nice little prize for their part in this farce.

How could Grandfather humiliate her this way?

She barely had time to absorb that when she got her next little jolt. Adam Barr was *not* one of her suitors after all. Instead, he'd come as her grandfather's agent.

Grandfather had tasked Adam with escorting her "beaus" to Texas, making sure everyone understood the rules of the game and then seeing that the rules were followed.

It was also his job to carry Jack back to Philadelphia if she balked at the judge's terms. Her grandfather would then pick out a suitable boarding school for the boy— robbing her of even the opportunity to share a home with him in Philadelphia.

Reggie cast a quick glance Adam's way, and swallowed hard. She had no doubt he would carry out his orders right down to the letter.

No! That would *not* happen. Even if it meant she had to face a forced wedding, she wouldn't let Jack be taken from her.

Will Regina find a way to outsmart her grandfather or will she fall in love with one of the bachelors?

Don't miss HANDPICKED HUSBAND by Winnie Griggs,

Available September 2012
wherever Love Inspired® Historical books are sold!

SHLIHEXP0912

4